Caught In The Middle

Caught In The Middle

BY

TRACY WILSON

http://beautifulpublications.com

Published by
Beautiful Publications LLC
Stratford, CT 06614

PRINT ISBN: 978-1-7343353-4-7
EBOOK ISBN: 978-1-7343353-5-4

Printed in the United States of America

Chapter 1

"Darien... Baby... I can explain..."

"I know everything I need to know..." he said as he put down the gun and began taking off his clothes...

"Darien... what are you doing?" Darien didn't answer me – he just finished getting undressed, got in the bed, and pulled the sheet back... "Darien..." I started to say...

"Come to bed..." he commanded. I didn't move. I just stood there and looked at him as Dexter stood behind me... "Come to bed... please..." he said as he held his arms open for me to climb in...

"Please... don't hurt me... I'm sorry..." I whispered as I started crying...

"I'm not here to hurt you... I'm here to join you..."

"What?"

"Please... come to bed and – what's your name?" he asked...

"Dexter..."

"Dexter... please... join us..."

"Darien... no..." I whispered as I shook my head...

"Lacey... I've been watching you with Dexter for about 15 minutes..."

"You were watching?"

"Yes..."

"Ummm – I'ma get dressed and go..." Dexter said...

"Why would you do that Dexter? You enjoy being with my wife – don't you?"

"I'm sorry..."

"No need to apologize..."

"Ummm... I don't understand..."

"Please... come to bed... and bring Dexter..." Darien insisted. I didn't want to. I was embarrassed and ashamed. As much as I wanted Dexter, I never wanted to be caught – not like this. I looked at Darien as I went closer to the bed. I was scared to death but as long as the gun was within reach, I was going to do whatever he asked..."

"I missed you..." he breathed as he pulled me up underneath him and held me... "Dexter?"

"Ummm... yes?"

"Are you married?"

"Ummm... no..."

"I wouldn't ask – but since you're wearing a condom, I was curious..."

"Oh... I wear condoms for protection..."

"Protection from what?"

"STDs..."

"Are you fucking anyone besides my wife?"

"Ummm... no..."

"Do you think my wife's a whore?" Darien asked as he raised his voice...

"No..."

"So... you're not fucking anyone else..." he said and then he pulled my face to his and kissed me... "And you don't think my wife's a whore..." he said and then he kissed me again... "So why are you really wearing a condom?"

"I didn't want to get her pregnant..."

"Well isn't that nice!"

"Ummm Sir... I really need to go..."

"Nonsense – come – join us – and take off that condom – I wanna see my competition...

"Ummm... I'm not with this..." Dexter said as he started to walk out the room...

"Uh, uh, uh..." Darien said as he picked up the gun and pointed it at him...

"Okay... I'll join you..." Dexter said as he climbed in bed beside me...

"That's better..." Darien said as he pulled me into another kiss... "Now Lacey... I'm going to ask you a question... and I need you to be honest... can you do that?" he asked as he ran his hands over my breasts and down between my legs...

"Yyyeesss..." I stuttered...

"How long as this been going on?" he asked as he took my left nipple in his mouth and sucked while massaging my right breast...

"A... a few... months..." I answered as I started crying...

"Lacey..." he breathed as he kissed my eyes... "Don't cry – I'm not going to hurt you..."

"Okay..." I breathed...

"Dexter – kiss her..." Dexter pulled my face to his and kissed me as Darien put his hand between my legs and started playing with my pussy... "You're wet..." he said and then he pulled his fingers out and licked them... "Mmmm... just like I like it – Dexter – taste her..." Dexter stopped kissing me and slid down the bed beside me and Darien watched intently as Dexter spread my lips with his tongue and began licking and sucking...

"Ooohhh..." I moaned...

"You like that – don't you Lacey?"

"Yes..."I moaned...

"Dexter – make her cum..." he commanded as he pulled my face to his, pushed his tongue in my mouth, and tongued me down...

"Haah... haah... haah... haah..."I moaned in his mouth as Dexter got up, pulled my legs apart, and dove in... "Haah... Haah... Haah... Haah..."

"Yes Dexter... that's it..." Darien said as he kissed me hard and played with my breasts. Dexter stuck his tongue inside me and began swirling it around while sucking...

"Aaah...   Aaah...   Aaah...   Aaah... AAAAAGH!"

4

"There it is..." Darien breathed as he looked at me... "Dexter – come lay beside Lacey..." Dexter did as he was told and Darien got up, got on top of me, spread my legs, and eased himself inside me... "Yeesss..." he moaned...

"Darien..." I moaned as he started thrusting...

"Yes... Darien..." he breathed as he fucked me. Dexter pulled my face to his and stuck his tongue in my mouth, tongued me down, and guided my hand to his dick...

"Huh... Huh... Huh... Huh..." I moaned in Dexter's mouth as Darien spread my legs and fucked me harder...

"Ugh! Ugh! Ugh! Ugh!" he grunted as I jerked Dexter's dick...

"Huh! Huh! Huh! Huh!

"Uggh! Uggh! Uggh! Uggh!"

"Ummph! Ummph! Ummph! Ummph!"

"That's it Lacey – gimmie me that pussy!" Darien growled as he threw my legs up on his shoulders and fucked me deeper...

"Huuh! Huuh! Huuh! Huuh! HHUUUUHH!"

"Uugh! Uugh! Uugh! Uugh! UUUUGGHH!"

"Umph! Umph! Umph! Umph! UUMMPPHH!" Darien collapsed on top of me and began licking and sucking my breasts as Dexter and I continued tonguing each other down. Darien pulled my face away from Dexter and tongued me down while he was still inside me...

"How did that feel?" Darien breathed as he kissed me...

"It was good..." I breathed...

"Dexter?"

"Ummm... yes?"

"Did you enjoy my wife?"

"Yes..." he breathed...

"Have you ever fucked my wife without a condom?"

"Ummm... no..." Darien pulled out of me, lay down beside me, and propped himself up on his elbow...

"Would you like to?"

"Ummm..."

"Lacey?"

"Yes?"

"How 'bout Dexter fucks you in your pussy..." he breathed in my ear... "While I fuck you in your ass?"

"No... I don't want to... please don't... I'll never do it again – I swear..."

"Lacey... please..." he breathed in my ear... "I won't hurt you... I promise..."

"Naa... she said no..." Dexter said...

"Lacey... please... for me..."

"You promise you won't hurt me?"

"I promise..." he breathed as he spread my cheeks and put the tip of his dick near my asshole...

"Okay..." I breathed...

"Lacey – you don't have to do this..." Dexter said as he pulled me to him and kissed me...

"It's okay..." I breathed as I moved my hand down to Dexter's ass and pushed him close to me...

"Lacey..." Darien breathed in my ear as he put the tip of his dick in my ass. Darien continued to ease himself in my ass slowly as Dexter began easing himself inside my pussy...

"Ooohhh..." I moaned. My ass was tight but once Dexter started thrusting I began to feel the sensation of both dicks and it felt good... "Huh... Huh... Huh... Huh..." I moaned...

"Lacey... fuck... your ass feels so good..." Darien breathed in my ear. Dexter pulled me to him, held me, and kissed me deeply as they both fucked me simultaneously...

"Uggh! Uggh! Uggh! Uggh!

"Huh... Huh... Huh... Huh...

"Umph... Umph... Umph... Umph..." I was coming inside and out and it was intense...

"AAGH! AAGH! AAGH! AAGH!"

"UGGH! UGGH! UGGH! UGGH!"

"UMPH! UMPH! UMPH! UMPH!"

"AAAAGGGGHHHH!"

"UUUUGGGGHHHH!"

"UUUMMMPPPHHH!" I fell asleep between the two of them as Darien kissed my neck, Dexter kissed my mouth, and their cum ran out my pussy and my ass.

Chapter 2

"Lacey..." Dexter whispered...

"Huh?" I answered sleepily..."

"I'm gonna go – I'll see you later..." he whispered again and then he bent down to kiss me...

"Okay..." I sighed as I watched him slip out...

"Honey..." I whispered as I touched Darien on the shoulder...

"Uuuggghhh..." he groaned as he stretched... "What time is it?"

"It's a little after 7..."

"That's gives me an idea..." he breathed as he pushed me down on my back and kissed me...

"Mmmm... don't you have to get ready for work?"

"You're not trying to get rid of me – are you?"

"Never..." I breathed as I pulled him into a kiss...

"So you still want me?"

"Oh Darien – Baby I'm sorry..."

"Do you love him?" I didn't want to answer him... "Look at me..." he said as he turned my face to him and looked me in my eyes...

"Yes..." I answered as I teared up...

"Thank you..." he breathed as he kissed me...

"For what?"

"For being honest with me..." he answered as he got up out of bed...

"Where are you going?"

"I'm going to get in the shower – care to join me?"

"Okay..." I smiled as I jumped up out of bed and followed him into the bathroom. Darien turned on the shower, waited for the water to get hot, got in, and started washing himself. I got in and stood in front of him underneath the shower head as the water ran down on my head. Darien turned me around, spread my legs, spread my cheeks, and began fucking me in my ass... "Darien..." I moaned...

"Uggh! Uggh! Uggh! Uggh!" Darien held me around my waist and kissed the back of my neck as he slowed down, but didn't stop...

"Darien..." I moaned again...

"Lacey..." he breathed in my ear as he started fucking me harder... "Fuck... I'm cumming... UUUGGGHHH!" I stood there with my legs spread apart as Darien continued holding me and kissing me on my neck... "I've wanted this for so long..." he breathed in my ear...

"I know..."

"Turn around..." he breathed. I turned around, stood still, and waited. Darien took the shampoo, opened it, squeezed some in his hands, put the shampoo back in the holder, and began massaging my scalp and hair...

"Oh Darien... that feels good..." I breathed. Darien rinsed my hair, opened the conditioner, squeezed some in his hands, put the conditioner back in the holder, and began massaging my scalp again... "Ooohhh..." Darien pulled me close to him, kissed me hard, and put his tongue in my mouth as he ran his hands up and down my back... "Mmmm..." Darien took the body wash with one hand, opened it, and squeezed it on me with one hand while holding me with the other. He put the body wash back in the holder and began rubbing it all over me... "Ooohhh..." Darien continued rubbing me all over, paying special attention to my breasts... "Oh Darien..." I moaned as he took my left breast in his mouth while squeezing the right one...

"Spread your legs..." he breathed and then he took my right breast in his mouth and began playing with my pussy...

"Darien... yes..." I moaned as he pushed his fingers inside me...

"Don't you dare cum..." he growled in my ear as he continued finger-fucking me...

"Darien... I'm gonna cum..." I moaned. Darien stopped suddenly and pulled out his fingers. I watched Darien take the bottle of body wash and squeeze some on his dick... "Let me..." I breathed as I began stroking his dick...

"Lacey..." he breathed as he closed his eyes and bent his head back...

"Don't you dare cum..." I laughed as I laid my head on his chest and continued stroking his dick...

"That's it!" he growled as he pushed me back against the shower, spread my legs, and thrust himself inside me...

"DARIEN!" I screamed...

"Yes Lacey – say my name!" he growled as he fucked me hard...

"Haah... Haah... Haah... Haah..."

"That's it Lacey... cum all over me..."

"I'M CUMMING... I'M CUMMING... I'M CUMMING... I'M CCUUMMIINNGG!"

"Say my name..." he breathed...

"Darien... Darien... Darien..."

"FFFUUUCCCKKK!"

"I love you..."

"I love you too..." he breathed as he pulled me into a kiss and kissed me hard... "I'm going to make coffee – I'll see you when you get out..." he said and then he grabbed a towel and hurried out the bathroom. I stepped out the shower, grabbed a towel, wrapped my hair, grabbed another towel, wrapped it around me, and walked into the kitchen... "Here..." Darien said as he placed the cup on the table and I sat down...

"Thank you..." I said as I sat down, picked up the coffee, and sipped...

"We need to talk..." he said as he began making omelets...

"I know..." I sighed...

"Why'd you do it?"

"I'm sorry..." I whispered as I started crying. Darien put down the bowl he was scrambling the eggs in, put down the fork, and came over to me...

"Stand up..." I did as I was told... "Come here..." he said as he pulled me into a hug...

"I'm sorry..." I cried...

"Lacey – listen to me..." he breathed as he kissed me...

"Okay..."

"I know you're sorry – and I forgive you..."

"Oh Darien – I love you so much..."

"I love you too – but I need you to listen..."

"Okay..."

"We need to talk..."

"I know... but..."

"Uh uh – stop doing that..."

"Okay..."

"We need to talk about this so we can get past it..."

"Okay..."

"That means when I ask you a question – I need you to answer me – and I need you to be honest with me..."

"Okay..."

"Now I want you to sit down, drink your coffee, and answer my question while I finish making breakfast..."

"Okay..." I sighed as I sat down and Darien went back to making the omelets... "I was at the gym and he came in..."

"Go on..." he said as he got the cheese out the refrigerator, put it in a bowl, and started grating it...

"He'd work out and we'd make jokes about him..."

"What kind of jokes?"

"Ummm... sex..."

"Was he the only man in the gym?" he asked as he put the cheese in the eggs, scrambled it together, and then poured it in the pan...

"No..." I sighed...

"He came to the gym – dressed to work out – and he made sure you could see all his assets..."

"Yea..."

"And ⁻ he ease-dropped on your conversations – and of all the women in the gym – he approached you..."

"Well... kinda..."

"He'd talk with the other women here and there – but he set his sights on you..." he said as he put two plates on the table, sat down, and gave me a fork...

"Thank you..." I breathed as I cut into the omelet and tasted it...

"How is it?"

14

"It's delicious..."

"Good..."

"What makes you think he set his sights on me?"

"Because..." he answered before tasting his omelet... "I was that guy..."

"I don't understand..."

"It seemed completely innocent at first – but one day – you were coming out of the shower – you had a towel on – you thought everyone was gone – you dropped your towel – you started getting dressed – he came in with nothing on but a towel..."

"Oh my God..." I whispered...

"He told you he thought everyone was gone – he was so sorry – he didn't mean to make you uncomfortable – he reached out to touch you on your shoulder – his towel fell off – and before you had a chance to react he had his hands all over you – right?"

"Yes..." I whispered...

"You didn't object so he picked you up, ripped off your panties, wrapped your legs around his waist – and fucked you – so tell me – was it in the shower or on the bench?"

"On the bench..." I sighed as I covered my face with my hands. Darien put down his fork and took my hands away from my face...

"Look at me..."

"No... I can't..."

"Look at me Lacey..."

"How could I have been so stupid?" I asked with tears in my eyes...

"Stop crying..." he said as he wiped my tears... "I need you to listen to me..."

"Okay..."

"I was that guy..."

"You were?"

"Yes..."

"Why?"

"Before I met you – that's what I did..."

"You went to the gym to meet women?"

"I went to the gym to prey on married women..."

"Are you saying Dexter set me up because I'm married?"

"Yes..."

"Why? Out of all the women that go to the gym – why me?"

"Because we don't go to the gym looking for a relationship..."

"I'm confused..."

"A single woman is going to become attached – she's going to expect a commitment – she'll expect you to be exclusive – that's not what we want – that's not what I wanted..."

"What did you want?"

"I wanted pussy – nothing more – nothing less – that's why I went for married women..."

"Oh my God – how could you do that?"

"I wasn't the one that took those vows – I didn't give a fuck about her husband – as long as

I got what I wanted and she was willing – I'd give her all the dick she could stand until she ended it – and then I'd move on to the next..."

"Oh my God – Darien – I'm sorry – I didn't mean to..."

"Yes you did..." he interrupted...

"I swear – I didn't..."

"Stop talking before you make me hurt you..." he said as he put his finger to my mouth... "You were excited – you got caught up in the moment – you fucked him – and you liked it – isn't that right?" I shook my head yes to acknowledge he was right as I started crying again... "I told you – I was that guy – I had many women – I was in their houses too – their husbands were completely clueless – their wives were sexually deprived and they were mine for the taking – so I took them every time they offered themselves to me – but what happened yesterday – with you – well..."

"Why?"

"As I told you – I was watching you for about 15 minutes..."

"Darien – please – let me..."

"I'm not done talking..."

"Okay..."

"My first thought was to blow his fuckin' head off in front of you – but since I've been that guy myself – I decided to join you..."

"I was afraid..."

"I know you were – but it wasn't about you – it was about him – and he fell for it – actually – he fell for you – and I can't have that..."

"I don't understand..."

"I was that man – and I never fell for a married woman – and even if I had – I would've never agreed to what happened yesterday..."

"You had a gun... you wouldn't let him leave..."

"Lacey – I'm a man – and as a man – I'm going out fighting – and he didn't even try to put up a fight!" he laughed...

"He didn't want to get shot..."

"Lacey – stop – I can't..." he laughed...

"Stop laughing at me!" I snapped...

"Lacey – I love you..." he said as he kissed me... "I forgive you – but right now – I don't give a fuck about your feelings – I need you to understand what I'm telling you..."

"Damn – that's fucked up..."

"Lacey – I need you to understand – I know I hurt your feelings – but you broke my heart..."

"I'm sorry..." I said as I started crying again...

"Lacey – he didn't put up a fight because he loves you..."

"What?"

"I watched him kiss you – I watched him taste you – I watched him make love to you – he made two fatal mistakes..."

"Two?"

"First – he fell for the mark..."

"So I was nothing more than a mark..." I sighed...

"Did you really think it was more than that?"

"Yes..." I sighed...

"Wow – I'm disappointed – but he made you fall in love with him so he still has some skills..."

"Oh my God – you make me sound like a whore..."

"I never called you a whore Lacey..."

"So he thinks I'm a whore?"

"Lacey – I need you to focus!"

"Okay..."

"If I ever got caught by the husband – I would never, ever, ever agree to a threesome with them..."

"What would you have done?"

"I would've gone out like a man..."

"So you would've risked being shot?"

"Hell yea – but Dexter thinks I'm cool with you being with him – and he loves you – and that's a problem..."

"I'll never see him again..."

"That's not good enough..."

"Please –tell me what you want – I'll do anything..."

"You'll do nothing..." he breathed as he kissed me...

"I don't understand..."

"When he contacts you – you tell him it's over..."

"I will – I promise..."

"And then you tell me..."

"Okay..."

"Now – I know this is going to be hard... but I need to ask you something..."

"Okay..."

"Did you suck his dick?"

"No..."

"Are you telling me the truth?"

"Yes..."

"Did you always use a condom?"

"Yes..."

"How many times was he in our bed?"

"Yesterday was the first time..." I answered as I started crying again. Darien came over to me, sat down, and took my face in his hands...

"I know this is hard... but I need to know..."

"I know..."

"What did you need that I didn't give you?"

"Darien... please... it wasn't your fault... it was me..."

"Yes... it was you... but you haven't answered my question..."

"I don't know... I just..."

"I thought you were going to be honest with me..."

"I'm sorry..."

"Lacey – I love you – but you're making me angry..." he said as he began squeezing my face..."

"Darien... please... you're hurting me..."

"I'm sorry – I don't mean to hurt you – but I need you to answer my question..." he said as he wiped my tears with his thumbs...

"I was... lonely..."

"You were lonely?"

"I wanted you..."

"I was right here..."

"You come home... we eat dinner... we cuddle... we go to bed... you turn over... you go to sleep..."

"So you felt like I didn't want you..."

"Yes..."

"Thank you for telling me..." he said as he let go of my face, got up, and left me in the kitchen.

Chapter 3

"Hello Darien..." Basil answered...

"Heeeyyyyy...." Darien slurred...

"Darien – you good?"

"I'm just great..."

"You been drinkin'?"

"Yeesss..."

"Where are you?"

"I'm at the bar..."

"Thirty-Three?"

"Yea – Bar 3 Thirty-three..."

"I'm on my way..." Bazil said as he hung up... "I gotta go check on Darien – I'll be back..." he said as he pulled Beautiee into a kiss...

"Hurry back..."

"I'll try..." Bazil said as he hurried out the door...

"Hey Lacey..." Beautiee answered...

"Can I come over?" I cried...

"Oh my God – what happened?"

"I fucked up!"

"I'll see you when you get here..."

Bazil walked into the bar and saw Darien sitting there by himself... "HeyBazil! Come have a drink with your friend! Bartender – two shots – and whatever he wants!"

"Hey Darien – what are we celebrating?"

"What are we celebrating? Hey bartender – he wants to know what we're celebrating – Aahaaaaaa... Ahaaaaaa!"

"Here's your shots – what can I get you sir – oh shit – you're Bazil Osgood!"

"Yes I am..." Bazil acknowledged...

"Damn right he's Bazil Osgood – and he's my friend! We go waaaaaayyyyy back – ain't that right Bazil?"

"Yes Darien – that's right – c'mon – let's go get a booth..."

"We ain't getting' shit until you drink your shot!"

"Okay – here we go – here's to my friend..."

"To friends!" Darien slurred as they drank...

"What can I get you?" the bartender asked...

"Bring me some henney..." Bazil answered... "C'mon Darien – let's get some food in you..." Bazil said as he helped Darien up off the stool and walked him over to the booth and sat him down...

"Welcome to Bar 3 Thirty-Three – would you like to hear tonight's specials?" the waitress asked...

"Just bring us burgers and fries..."

"You got it..." the waitress said and then she went to place the order...

"Beautiee..." I cried as soon as she opened the door...

"Girl – come here..." she said as she pulled me into a hug...

"I fucked up..."

"Come sit down in the living room..."

"Okay..." After we got in the living room I sat down on the couch and looked around...

"What do you need?' Beautiee asked...

"I need a drink..."

"I have moscato..."

"That ain't strong enough..."

"Well we have henney – but you haven't eaten so I wouldn't advise it..."

"Beautiee – you know what – le'me go..."

"Don't you dare leave – wait there – I'll be back..." she said as she left to go in the kitchen. When she came back I got an instant attitude...

"What the fuck is this?"

"It's a sandwich..."

"I don't want a fuckin' sandwich! I want a fuckin' drink!"

"And you'll get a fuckin' drink as soon as you eat this fuckin' sandwich..." Beautiee laughed...

"Gimmie the sandwich..." I laughed as I snatched the plate from her and started eating...

"Here's your burgers – can I get you something to drink?" the waitress asked...

"Hell yea!" Darien slurred...

"We'll get something to drink after we eat..." Bazil laughed...

"You lucky I love you..." Darien laughed as he started eating...

"What happened?"

"She's been fuckin' him for five months..."

"Damn... I'm sorry..."

"I love her so much..."

"She loves you too..."

"She said that..."

"Trust me – she loves you..."

"Why'd she do it man?"

"Because she's not perfect... she made a mistake..."

"You full of shit – you wouldn't be sayin' that shit if it was Beautiee..."

"It was Beautiee..."

"Oh shit!"

"Okay – I ate the sandwich – can I have a drink now – please?"

"Yes Lacey..." Beautiee laughed as she took the plate from me...

"I'ma follow you this time..." I laughed as I got up to follow her into the kitchen. Beautiee went over to the counter, took down a glass, poured me some Hennessey, handed it to me, and I gulped it down..."

"Okay that's it – what happened?"

"I got caught..."

"You got caught? Doing what?"

"Darien came home early..."

"Lacey!"

"I know, I know!" I cried..."

"Beautiee cheated on me and then she left me..."

"Oh damn! What the fuck did you do?"

"I cheated on her so she cheated on me to get revenge..."

"Oh shit – now I remember..." Darien sighed...

"What happened?"

"I came home early... I saw them... I had my gun drawn..."

"Darien – no!"

"He's alive... she's alive..."

"So what did you do with the gun?"

"I got undressed and told them I was there to join them..."

"Oh shit! What?"

"Yea..."

"So did you fuck him?"

"Hell no!"

"Oh so you both fucked Lacey?"

"Yea..."

"You're a better man than me..."

"I'm a fool in love..."

"You're not a fool in love – you're in love – and he's crazy!"

"Poor thing has no idea what's coming..." Darien laughed...

"You're scaring me..." Bazil said...

"Yea – they were scared too..."

"Scared or not – you would've had to shoot me!" Bazil laughed...

"That's what I told Lacey..."

"Huh?"

"I told Lacey how men like him – like me – prey on married women – and give them the dick until they tell us it's over – but he made Lacey fall in love with him..."

"Damn..."

"And he loves her too..."

"She told you that?"

"She didn't have to – I watched him kiss her, taste her, make love to her..."

"Sorry man..."

"I'm not..."

"You're not?"

"Naa – it'll make it easier for me to kill him..."

"Don't talk like that..."

"What would you do if it was Beautiee?"

"I'd kill him..."

"Okay then..."

"I don't know if I could've done that..."

"Bullshit – you've had threesomes before..."

"Yes – I've had threesomes with two women – I don't think I could handle it if Beautiee wanted another man..."

"I didn't think I could either – but she enjoyed it... and I enjoyed that ass..."

"So you finally tapped that ass huh?"

"Yea..." Darien smiled to himself..."

"I tapped Beautiee's ass too..."

"Yea? She like it?"

"You already know how I get down..."

"Yea – I do – that's why Lacey started fuckin' Dexter in the first place..."

"Huh?"

"I'm not like you – I can't fuck all day and night!"

"Wait a minute – how often do you and Lacey have sex?"

"A couple a times a week..."

"You need to see a doctor about that..."

"I don't have a problem gettin' it up!" Darien snapped...

"Your sex drive is too low – you should be fuckin' Lacey's brains out..."

"Okay – since you know so much – what the fuck am I supposed to tell my doctor?"

"Tell the doctor you're there for a check up – they'll check your testosterone as part of your check up..."

"Oh hell no – ain't nobody goin' in my ass man!"

"They don't go in your ass for that man!"
Bazil laughed... "But they will stick a finger in
there and check your prostate..."

"See? I knew it!"

"It's not a big deal – when he says he
wants to check your prostate – tell him you want
to lay on your side on the table –it doesn't last
long..."

"You get yours checked?"

"Oh yea..."

"Come sit down..." Beautiee said and then
we went over to the table... "What happened?"

"He came home early... I didn't know he
was watching us..."

"He was watching you?"

"He watched us before he came in the room
with the gun..."

"Oh my God! Is he dead?"

"Not yet..."

"Lacey – what did he do?"

"Have you ever had a threesome?"

"Yea..."

"Why'd you do it?"

"Le'me get us a drink..." Beautiee laughed
as she got up to go pour us drinks and then she
came back to the table...

"Okay – tell me..." I said...

"Drink!" Beautiee commanded. I gulped
my drink down as she gulped down hers...
"Well..." she sighed... "Bazil cheated on me..."

"Beautiee! You never told me that!"

"So I cheated on him to get revenge – but that only made me feel worse – so I left him..."

"You left Bazil? Oh wow – you must've been devastated..."

"I was – but I was only gone a week..." she laughed...

"Where'd you go?"

"I went to the bank, withdrew some money, and broke down crying – next thing you know – I'm at Friday's drinking Long Island Ice Teas with Sonia..."

"Sonia?"

"She handled Bazil's accounts..."

"Oh shit! Did you clean him out?"

"It wasn't about the money..."

"So what was it then?"

"That's not relevant – I was in pain – Sonia gave me a shoulder to cry on – and then she went into how she chose to be with women because of how her mother was treated..."

"So she thinks men ain't shit – well it's not just men – we cheat too..."

"Exactly – that's how I wound up having a threesome..."

"Wait – I don't get it..."

"I was with Sonia for a week..."

"Oh my God! What was it like?"

"It was nice..."

"Wow..."

"So when I came back, Bazil asked me if I enjoyed it – next thing you know – we invited her over..."

"That's kinda what happened yesterday..." I sighed...

"What happened Lacey?" Beautiee asked as she touched my hand...

"He got undressed... he said he wasn't there to hurt us... he said he was there to join us..."

"Oh damn – I don't think Bazil would do that..."

"I didn't think Darien would either... but he had the gun... and..." I couldn't finish – I burst into tears...

"Oh my God – Lacey... did he rape you?"

"No... but..."

"You enjoyed it... and now you feel guilty..."

"Yea..."

"Are you going to see him again?"

"Hell no – especially after what Darien told me..."

"What did Darien tell you?"

"He told me how he was just like Dexter – he went to the gym to prey on married women – he said I was nothing more than a mark – but I love him..." I explained as I started crying...

"Oh Lacey..."

"I know – I hurt my husband – and I played myself – I can't believe I was so fuckin' stupid!"

"Lacey – it's gonna be okay..." Beautiee said as she held me...

"Darien told me Dexter loves me..."

"What makes him think that?"

"He said Dexter made two fatal mistakes..."

"What mistakes?"

"He said Dexter fell for the mark – I feel so stupid..." I cried...

"What makes him so sure Dexter loves you?"

"Because he didn't fight to get away from the gun..."

"Bazil would shoot a mutha fucka..."

"He thought about it – believe me..."

"What was the other mistake?"

"He said Dexter thinks Darien is okay with us – and he's not..."

"Oh damn..."

"That's not the worst part..." I sighed...

"Damn Lacey – what else is there?"

"He asked me what did I need that he didn't give me... he made me tell him why... I didn't want to..."

"Lacey – he needed to know..."

"I told him I was lonely – he comes home – we eat – we cuddle – he turns over – he goes to sleep..."

"Well at least you told him..."

"He said thank you for telling me – and then he left!" I exclaimed as I cried on Beautiee's shoulder...

"Lacey – he didn't leave you..."

"Yes he did!" I cried...

"He's with Bazil..."

"He is?" I sniffed...

"Bazil went to go see him before you got here..."

"I hurt him so bad..."

"He'll forgive you..."

"He said he does..."

"Now comes the hard part..."

"The hard part?"

"He forgives you – now you have to forgive yourself..."

"How am I supposed to do that?"

"Girl – I just figured that out myself..." Beautiee sighed...

"That long?"

"I went through it – I used to ask Bazil how could he still love me..." she sighed...

"Damn – I'm in for it huh?"

"Yea – but Darien will help you – as long as you never do it again..."

"Oh no – I'm done – this shit is not for me!" I laughed...

"I do have a suggestion though..."

"What Beautiee – tell me..."

"Have another threesome with a woman – and make it about him..."

"Beautiee! What the hell makes you think I'd do that?"

"It worked for us..." she answered as she poured us another drink.

Chapter 4

"Hey Beautiee – I'm home..." I sighed...

"Good – don't do anything crazy..."

"What – like drink a bottle of moscato and cry myself to sleep?"

"Girl – I've been there..."

"Okay – you've been there – since you know so much – what the fuck should I do then?"

"The first thing you need to do is lose the attitude before you lose a friend..."

"I'm sorry..."

"It's okay – I still love you..." she laughed...

"Thank you – I don't know what I'd do without you..."

"I've been there too..."

"You keep saying that..."

"Girl – the stories I could tell – but this isn't about me – it's about you – and Darien..."

"Why do you do that?"

"Do what?"

"You never wanna talk about you and Bazil..."

"What else do you need to know besides what I wrote in my book?"

"Okay – how did you get through it? Did you have somebody to talk to besides Bazil?"

"Keisha..."

"Keisha? Your neighbor?"

"Yea..."

"Okay – besides Keisha – what else did you do?"

"I fucked him every chance I got..."

"So you never got drunk? You never got high?"

"I didn't say that..." she laughed...

"I knew it!"

"I love my moscato and I smoke once in a while – but when I wasn't talking to Keisha I was fuckin' my husband..."

"I don't know if I can do that..."

"Why not?"

"Darein's not like Bazil..."

"What makes you think that?"

"Don't get me wrong – he's got good dick... but..."

"What Lacey?"

"He doesn't want me like that..." I sighed...

"Lacey – le'me ask you something..."

"Okay..."

"What happened after you woke up today?"

"We took a shower, he made coffee, we talked, we had breakfast – you know the rest..."

"That's it?"

"We fucked in the shower – are you happy – damn!" I laughed...

"Yes! That's what I'm talkin' about!"

"I don't get it..."

"Girl! He fucked the shit outta you – right?"

"Damn you nosey!" I laughed...

"You wanna know what I did – that's what I did!"

"You let him fuck the shit outta you?"

"See – that's where we get fucked up – we have good men – we love them – we want them – they give good dick – and we can't admit we enjoy it – I don't let Bazil do shit I don't want him to do – and I want him to do everythang!"

"I didn't mean to offend you – I'm sorry..."

"You still don't get it!" she laughed...

"Get what?"

"When you say you let him – that implies that you only did what he wanted – it implies that you're complacent – it's like saying you don't really enjoy being with him..."

"Oooohhh..."

"Now you understand..."

"Oh yea... I understand alright..."

"I like what you're saying Lacey..."

"So will he..." I said and then I hung up...

"Shit – why is he texting me..." I sighed as I opened his message...

"Hey, I'm just checking on you. Are you okay?"

"Yes..."

"I need to see you..."

"Absolutely not..."

"Why not? Don't you want me?"

"I did... but I don't want you anymore..."

"I rocked your world and you know it..."

"That never should've happened..."

"Maybe not – but it did..."

"Don't remind me..."

"Why not? You enjoyed it... and so did I..."

"I want my husband..."

"That's not what you said last night..."

"What I said last night... the name I called... was Darien..."

"You called his name... but you wanted me..."

"I wish I never did..."

"I've invaded your body... I've invaded your mind... I've invaded your soul... and there's nothing you can do about it..."

"Do yourself a favor – find someone else..."

"I want you Lacey..."

"What about my husband?"

"I don't give a fuck about your husband... I never did..." I looked at the phone and read that over and over...

"How could you say that! You knew I was married..."

"You knew you were married the first time we fucked... you knew you were married every time we fucked... and it didn't stop you..."

"You're right – but I'm not doing that again..."

"I won't let you go... you're mine... and I'm yours... you told me you love me..."

"I wish I never told you that..."

"Does your husband know you love me?"

"Yes... I told him..."

"Wow – I'm surprised – how long do I have to wait?"

"Wait for what?"

"For you to leave your husband?"

"I'm not leaving my husband – it's over between us..."

"We'll see about that..."

"Hey..." Darien said as he came inside and locked the door..."

"Darien – we need to talk..."

"No... we don't..." he breathed as he pulled me into a kiss...

"Darien... wait..." I breathed as he began kissing me on my neck...

"No..." he breathed as he picked me up in his arms, and tossed me on the bed...

"You're drunk..." I laughed...

"I'm drunk... in love..." he breathed as he climbed on top of me, kissed me... and I bust out laughing...

"What's so funny?"

"I'm picturing Beyoncé and Jay-Z..." I laughed as I pulled Darien down on top of me...

"Is that right?" he breathed in my ear as he moved my shirt up, took my left breast out my bra, and began sucking...

"Ooohhh..." I moaned. Darien continued sucking as he unbuttoned my jeans, slid the zipper down, and put his hand in my panties...

"Darien..." I moaned as he moved his hand down and parted my lips with his fingers...

"Yes Lacey..." he breathed. Darien pushed my jeans and panties off my waist and then he stopped, got up on his knees, and snatched them off... "Sit up..." he commanded. I did as I was told. Darien pulled my shirt over my head, unclasped my bra, slid it off, and tossed it... "Lay back..." I did as I was told... "Close your eyes..." I did as I was told... "Spread your legs..." I did as I was told... "Are you ready?"

"Yeesss..." I breathed... and then I felt something...

"Ooohhh..." I moaned as he went across my breasts and down my body with the flogger...

"You've been naughty..." he said as he ran it between my legs...

"Ooohhh..." I moaned...

"You need to be punished..." he breathed as he came up on the bed, climbed on top of me, pushed his tongue in my mouth, and started tonguing me down...

"Mmmm... what's the safe word?"

"There isn't one..." he growled as he started kissing me down my body...

"Oh Darien..." I moaned...

"Yes Lacey..." he breathed and then he flicked his tongue on my clit..."

"Ooohhh..." I moaned and then he dove in... "DARIEN!" I screamed as he took my clit in his mouth and sucked it hard. I tried to back away from him but he grabbed me by my legs, stuck his tongue inside, and ran his nose back and forth across my clit as he tongue-fucked me... "Haah... Haah... Haah... Haah... HHAAGGHH!" I grabbed his head, arched my back, and came up off the bed as my legs shook but Darien was relentless... "Darien..." I panted... "It's... it's... sensitive..."

"Don't move..." he growled and then he went back to devouring me...

"Darien... Haah..." I wanted him to stop but at the same time – I didn't – it felt so good... he felt so good...

"There it is..." he breathed as he came up from between my legs and I saw my juices glistening from his chin. Darien picked up the flogger again and smacked me across my breasts with it...

"Ouch..."

"Did I hurt you?"

"A little..."

"Le'me see..." he breathed as he climbed on top of me, pushed himself up on his arms, and thrust himself inside me...

"Darien..." I moaned as I went to pull him in deeper...

"Uh uh... le'me see..." he growled. I put my hands down at my sides and spread my legs wider... "Yes –le'me see them titties bounce!" he growled as he continued fucking me...

"Haah... Haah... Haah... Haah..."

"Uuugh! Uuugh! Uuugh!"

"Darien... Darien... Darien..."

"Yes Lacey... cum for me..."

"I'M CCUUMMIINNGG! AAGGHH!"

"UUUGH! UUUGH! UUUGH! UUUGH! UUUGGGHHH!"

"FUCK!" I panted as Darien collapsed on top of me and I pulled him into a kiss...

"Let go of me..." he commanded...

"What's wrong?"

"I'm not done punishing you..." he breathed as he got up off me and picked up the flogger... "Get up on your knees..." I did as I was told... "Come here..." he breathed as he pulled me into a kiss. Darien pushed his tongue in my mouth, tongued me down, picked up the flogger, and smacked me on my ass...

"Mmmmph..." I moaned in his mouth. Darien stopped kissing me and looked at me before his next command...

"Get on your hands and knees – and take my dick in your mouth..." I did as he commanded... "Yes Lacey... suck my dick..." he commanded and then he picked up the flogger, ran it down my back, ran it across my ass, and smacked my ass with it as he pushed his dick in my mouth further...

"MMPPHH!" I moaned on his dick...

"Yes... suck it..." he growled and then he smacked my ass again...

"MMPPHH!" I moaned on his dick again. Darien fucked my mouth harder and smacked my ass with the flogger as his orgasm was building...

"MMMPH! MMMPH! MMMPH! MMMPH! MMMPH!"

"FFUUCCKK.... LLAACCEEYY!" Darien filled my mouth so full some of his cum leaked out before I could swallow it all... "God damn..." he breathed as I continued sucking him softly... "Lacey..."

"Yeesss..." I moaned on his dick...

"Come here..." I did as I was told. Darien pulled me into a hard kiss and held me... "I love you Lacey..."

"I love you too..."

"You hungry?"

"Yea..."

"C'mon – I'll come up with something..." he said as we got down off the bed and I followed him into the kitchen. Darien tied the apron around his dick and I watched his ass intently as he went in the refrigerator, took out the ground beef, onions, peppers, ricotta, and mozzarella...

"What are you making?"

"Stuffed shells..." he answered as he got a pot, filled it with water, poured some oil in it, and began chopping the onions and peppers into small bits. I got up, went over to him, and pushed myself against his ass as I held him and started kissing him on his back... "Do you want another spanking?" he asked as he continued chopping...

"Yes..." I whispered as I knelt down, grabbed his ass, and pushed his dick in my mouth...

"Lacey... stop..."

"No..."

"Lacey..." stop..."

"No..."

"Get up..." he commanded as he pulled me up by my hair...

"What's wrong?"

"Turn around..." he commanded. I did as I was told... "Put your hands on the counter and spread your legs..." I did as I was told... "Look at that..." he breathed as he cupped my ass and squeezed it..."

"I can't..." I laughed...

"Come with me..." he said as he pulled me from the kitchen into the bathroom towards the mirror...

"Oh wow..." I gasped as I looked in the mirror and saw the welts on my ass...

"You see that?" he breathed as he pulled me close to him...

"Yes..."

"How does this feel?" he breathed in my ear as he grabbed my ass in both hands...

"It feels good..." I breathed...

"Do you still want another spanking?"

"Yes..." I breathed...

"Good..." he said and then he pulled me back into the kitchen and went back over to the counter to finish chopping the onions and peppers. I knelt down, grabbed his ass, and pushed his dick in my mouth again – and this time – Darien grabbed my head with both hands and fucked my mouth... "Suck my dick!" he growled...

"MMMPH! MMMPH! MMMPH! MMMPH!"

"UUUGH! UUUGH! UUUGH! UUUGH! UUUGGGHHH!"

"Darien... the water..."

"Huh?"

"The water's boiling..."

"Oh okay..."he laughed. I got up and went to sit at the table as he put the shells in the water and then he bent down to take the frying pan out the cabinet, put it on the stove, turned the flame up, and put the onions and peppers in the pan... and I started laughing...

"What's so funny?"

"Well... when you said you were drunk in love... I pictured Beyoncé and Jay-Z... and..." I started laughing harder...

"Oh yea – she sucks dick..." he laughed. I sat there quiet as Darien put the ground beef in the pan, browned it with the onions and peppers, turned the flame off, drained the shells, and pre-heated the oven...

"Darien..." I sighed...

"Yes Lacey?"

"We need to talk..."

"Le'me get this in the oven – and then we'll talk..."

"Okay..." I watched Darien stuff the shells, line the baking pan with aluminum foil, pour the sauce over them, and put the pan in the oven. After he closed the oven door he came to sit at the table...

"Okay – let's talk..." he sighed...

"Please don't be mad at me..."

"Why would I be mad at you?"

"I need to tell you something..."

"Okay..."

"I didn't mean to..."

"Lacey – don't start that shit again..."

"Darien... please... let me finish..."

"Okay – go ahead..."

"I didn't mean to fall for him – I swear..."

"Why are you telling me this now?"

"Because – I tried to tell you yesterday – and you got angry..."

"I'm sorry..."

"It's okay – I understand..."

"No it isn't – I should've walked away..."

"You did... and I thought you weren't coming back..." I whispered as I started crying...

"Lacey..." he whispered as he wiped my tears... "I'm not going to leave you – I love you..."

"I love you too – and I need to be honest with you..."

"Tell me..."

"I don't want to hurt you..."

"Lacey – tell me..."

"He contacted me today..."

"So you were naughty..." 'Darien breathed as he pulled me into a kiss..."

"Darien... please..."

"Stop talking..." he breathed as he kissed me again...

"I'll change my number – I'll block him – I'll do whatever you want..."

"I want you to stop talking..."

"Okay..."

"I know..."

"You know? How?"

"I want you to keep doing what you're doing..."

"I'm not doing anything..."

"I'll take care of it..."

"What if he contacts me again?"

"He will – and when he does – you let me know..." he breathed as he kissed me again...

"I don't deserve you..."

"Uh uh – stop that before I give you another spanking..."

"You promise?" Darien didn't answer me – he just smiled at me mischievously and then he got up, went over to the oven, took the food out, fixed our plates, and brought them to the table...

"Have you ever done that before?"

"What?"

"Spanking..."

"No..."

"You have welts on your ass..."

"I know..."

"I didn't realize I hit you that hard..."

"It wasn't that hard – it just stung a little..."

"It stung a little... and you liked it..."

"Yea..." I sighed...

"I'm going to punish you more often..." he said as we finished eating.

Chapter 5

"Hey Lacey..." Beautiee answered...

"Beautiee..." I whispered...

"Why are you whispering?"

"Because I don't want Darien to hear me..."

"Oh God – are you alright?"

"Well..."

"Lacey – what's wrong?"

"Okay – remember when you said you fucked Bazil every chance you got?"

"I still do..." she laughed...

"Well... umm..."

"Lacey – where are you?" Darien called out...

"I'm in the bathroom..."

"Lacey – what's going on?" Beautiee asked...

"Did you ever get punished?"

"Oh yea..."

"You did?"

"Bazil punished me for denying him pussy..."

"Wait – you left him because he cheated on you!" I laughed...

"Yes – and when I came back, he told me I needed to be punished for denying him pussy..." she laughed...

"What is wrong with these men?" I laughed...

"So how'd you like being punished?"

"Okay – that's it..." Darien said as he got up out the bed and tip-toed to the bathroom...

"I loved it..."

"Me too..."

"It felt so good!"

"I know – Bazil told me if I ever left him again he'd fuck me to death – and after I went to prison he sure tried it!" Beautiee laughed...

"Wait a minute – that wasn't your fault!"

"Bazil said it didn't matter..."

"He hasn't fucked me like that in a long time..."

"I'm glad you're happy Lacey..."

"I am – I had to sneak in the bathroom to call you..."

"Oh damn – you're really getting punished!" she laughed...

"I told him I liked it..."

"Aww... that's beautiful..."

"It sure is..."

"Enjoy the ride girl..."

"I'm enjoying more than that!" I laughed...

"Bazil and I are in a really good place now..."

"Does Bazil ever bring it up?"

"No – but he was just as much at fault as I was..."

"This is all my fault..." I sighed...

"It will get better – just keep fuckin'..."

"Oh shit – he's comin' – I'm about to be on punishment again – bye!"

"Good morning..." Darien said and then he pulled me into a kiss...

"Mmmm... good morning..." I breathed...

"Who were you talking to?"

"I was talking to Beautiee..."

"How's she doing?"

"She's fine..."

"Why'd you come in here to talk to her?"

"I didn't want to disturb you..."

"I need to jump in the shower – I have an appointment..."

"Can I join you?"

"I'd love that – but if you join me – I won't get out the shower..."

"Okay..." I sighed...

"I'll make it up to you when I get home later..." he said and then he hurried into the shower...

"Good morning..." Bazil breathed as Beautiee kissed him awake...

"Good morning..." she breathed as she reached down between his legs...

"Beautiee – I can't..."

"Please..." she breathed as she began kissing him down his stomach...

"Beautiee... I'm sorry..."

"Okay..." she sighed...

"I have to get in the shower – I've got an appointment..." he said as he jumped up out of bed...

"I'll join you..."

"Beautiee – I can't – I'll make it up to you – I promise..." he said as he hurried into the shower...

I watched Darien get dressed. He was unusually quiet... "What time is your appointment?"

"9..."

"Are you coming right back?"

"I'll call you..." he said as he kissed me goodbye and hurried out the door...

"Bazil?"

"Yes Beautiee?"

"Is everything okay?"

"Everything's fine..." he answered as he got dressed...

"What time is your appointment?"

"9..."

"Are you coming right back?"

"Depends on how long it takes..." he said and then he kissed her goodbye and hurried out the door...

"Good morning – do you have an appointment?" the receptionist asked...

"Yes..."

"Your name?"

"Darien Beaufort..."

"Is this your first time here?"

"Yes..."

"Okay – I need you to fill out these forms and give them back to me – and I also need your insurance..."

"Okay – thank you..." Darien said as he sat down and started filling out the paperwork...

"Good morning Mr. Osgood – are you here to see Dr. Har?"

"Not today..."

"What brings you here then?"

"Bazil – over here..." Darien called out...

"Have a good day..." the receptionist said as Bazil went to sit with Darien...

"Good morning..."

"Good morning..." Darien said without picking his head up...

"It's just a check-up – relax..." Bazil whispered...

"I can't – I keep thinking about him playing with my ass and my dick!"

"You want me to go in there with you?"

"I can't ask you to do that..."

"I'll go with you..."

"Mr. Beaufort?" the receptionist called out...

"Yes?"

"Dr. Har will see you now..."

"Okay..." Darien said as they both got up...

"You can leave your insurance card with me..." she said as Darien gave her the clipboard and they both went to the back...

"Good morning Mr. Osgood – I didn't know you had an appointment today..."

"I don't – my friend does..."

"You must be Mr. Beaufort – I'm Dr. Dean Har – how are you?" he asked as he extended his hand...

"Nervous as hell..." Darien answered as he shook Dr. Har's hand...

"You've never had a prostate exam – have you?"

"No..."

"It's not that bad – by the time I make you uncomfortable – it's over..."

"That doesn't make me feel any better!" Darien exclaimed...

"Okay – tell me why you're here..."

"I'm here because... my wife..." Darien couldn't finish...

"When was the last time you had a physical?"

"Last year..."

"Okay – here's what I'm going to do – I'm going to give you a complete exam – and during the exam we're going to be close..."

"I know..."

"You're married – right?"

"Yes..."

"Your wife goes to the gynecologist – right?"

"Yes..."

"After today you'll have an idea of what she goes through..."

"You're not helping!" Darien exclaimed...

"You see this?" Dr. Har asked as he picked up a speculum...

"What the hell is that?"

"This is a speculum – you spread your legs, you put them up in stirrups, we put some gloves on, we put a little gel on it, we put it inside – and then we open it – like this..." Dr. Har explained as he started screwing it open...

"Oh hell no!" Darien exclaimed as Bazil covered his mouth to keep from laughing...

"After we take this out – you keep your legs open and we insert two fingers...

"Fuck this – I'm out!" Darien said as Bazil and Dr. Har bust out laughing...

"What the fuck are you laughing for?" Darien snapped...

"Mr. Beaufort – that's what your wife goes through every time she goes to the gynecologist..."

"Oh my God..."

"And that's just for the Vagina..."

"Huh?"

"After they check the vagina, they have to check her breasts – in a circular motion – like this..." he explained as he demonstrated on his chest...

"I had no idea..."

"Most men don't – but once I explain what their wives go through when they visit the gynecologist – they start to feel better about getting their prostate checked..."

"If she can go through all that for me – I guess I can do this for her..."

"Exactly..."

"I'ma go wait outside..." Bazil laughed as he opened the door and left...

"Do you need me to get undressed?" Darien asked...

"Not yet – let's talk..."

"Okay..."

"Do you drink?"

"Yes..."

"How often do you drink?"

"Every day..."

"How many drinks do you have per day?"

"I usually have a few drinks after dinner..."

"If your test results come back indicating that you have low testosterone – you need to reduce the amount of alcohol you drink..."

"I do?"

"Absolutely. Alcohol has serious effects on your testosterone – it can cause erectile dysfunction and it can also damage your testicle's ability to produce testosterone..."

"Damn – is it reversible?"

"Yes..."

"How?"

"If you stop drinking – your testosterone levels can return to normal..."

"So I can't drink again? Ever?"

"Let's not get ahead of ourselves – it may not be an issue for you – but as your doctor I'm advising you to reduce your intake if you're a heavy drinker..."

"Okay..."

"Come closer..."

"Ummm... okay..." Darien said as he leaned towards Dr. Har's face...

"I'm looking at your eyes..."

"Okay..."

"When you have cirrhosis of the liver – you get a yellowing of the eyes due to the accumulation of bilirubin in the blood..."

"I know someone who died from that..."

"You have nice eyes..."

"Thank you doctor..."

"Okay – now I wanna talk to you about testosterone..."

"Okay..."

"A normal testosterone level range for men is 300 to 1,000 per deciliter. After you turn 40, your level starts to decrease by 1 percent every year..."

"How do you test my testosterone levels?'

"The best way to test your levels is to do a blood test. They have home testing kits but those kits test your saliva – and sometimes you need a blood test to make sure the results are accurate..."

"Might as well just do a blood test..."

"Exactly – so you're going to get undressed and put a gown on with the opening to the front – and then I'll examine you..."

"Why do I need to get completely undressed?"

"I need to check your abdomen and your breasts..."

"My breasts?"

"In men it's actually called gynecomastia – an abnormal increase in breast tissue..."

"Oh so that's what that is..."

"'Yes..."

"I just thought it was fat..."

"Sometimes it is – but sometimes it's not – and when it's not, sometimes it's necessary to get a mammogram..."

"Oh shit!"

"Oh yea – men can get breast cancer too..."

"Damn!"

"I'm going to give you some privacy – get undressed, put this gown on, and sit on the table..."

"Okay..." Darien said as he got up and Dr. Har left the room. After Darien was ready he sat up on the table and waited...

"Can I come in?" Dr. Har asked...

"Yes doctor..."

"Okay – show me those eyes again..." Darien looked into the doctor's eyes as the doctor checked them with the light...

"I've never gazed into a man's eyes before..." Darien laughed...

"Turn your head..." Darien turned his head and the doctor checked one ear and then the other... "Tilt your head back..." Darien tilted his head back and the doctor checked his nose... "Open wide and say aaahhh..."

"Aaah..." Darien said as the doctor stuck the tongue depressor in his mouth and checked his throat...

"Stick out your tongue..." Darien did as he was told... "Okay – I'm going to take your blood pressure, draw some blood, and then we'll get to why you're really here..."

"Okay..." Darien sighed...

Chapter 6

Dr. Har checked Darien's blood pressure, took some blood, and collected the tubes... "I'm going to have this sent to the lab – and then I'll be back..." he said as he left the room. When he came back in the room, Darien got nervous... "Ummm... you okay?"

"Do you get... you know..."

"Yes I get my prostate checked every year..."

"Okay..."

"I need you to lie down..." he said as he washed his hands...

"Okay..."

"I'm putting on gloves – see?" he said as he put on the gloves...

"I see..."

"I need you to put your arms above your head so I can check your chest – you can put them underneath your head if you like..."

"Okay..."

"So far, so good..." Dr. Har said as he felt around...

"Now I'm going to push on your abdomen..." he said as he started pushing on his abdomen... "Any tenderness?"

"Nope..."

"Okay – I'm going to check your testicles and your penis..."

"Ummm..."

"I'm not going anywhere near your ass..."

"Okay..."

"Your testicles look normal – I'm going to check for any abnormalities – it'll just take a sec..." he said as he felt one and then the other...

"I'm going to check your penis..." he said as he took the penis in his hand...

"Ummm... what are you looking for?"

"Discoloration, bumps, abnormal size..."

"Abnormal size?"

"I'll explain that in a minute – I need you to turn on your side..." he said as he helped Darien turn on his side... "I'm going to put some gel on my fingers - see?" he said as he showed Darien the gel...

"Yea..."

"Okay – I'm going to spread your cheeks, slide my finger, in, check your prostate, and pull my finger out – don't shit in my hand..."

"Oh my God!" Darien laughed...

"Made you laugh..." Dr. Har said as he inserted his finger in Darien's ass...

"Oh God..."

"I'm done!"

"Thank God!"

"That wasn't too bad – right?" he asked as he helped Darien sit up...

"Naaa..."

"Good..."

"Has anyone ever shit in your hand?"

"I'll let you in on a secret..."

"Okay..."

"I've never had a patient shit in my hand – but whenever I check the prostate on a gay patient – they ejaculate on the table..."

"Oh my God!" Darien exclaimed as he bust out laughing...

"Get dressed – I'll be back in a few minutes..." he said as he left the room...

"Thank God that's over..." Darien said as he got dressed and waited for Dr. Har to come back. When he came back in the room he sat at the table...

"Okay – first – everything looks good – your prostate feels normal..."

"Okay..."

"The reason I check the penis is because just like you can have low testosterone – you can also have too much testosterone – this is known as congenital adrenal hyperplasia – CAH. This can result in having an abnormally large penis and a very deep voice..."

"I wonder if Barry White had that..."

"Your penis is fine..."

"Really?"

"Having a big dick is normal – most black men have big dicks – but a few have abnormally large ones – I have one patient that gives his wife an episiotomy every time they have sex..."

"An episiotomy?"

"See this area right here?" Dr. Har asked as he pointed to the chart of a man lying with his legs open...

"Yea..."

"Every time he has sex with his wife – he tears it..."

"Ooohh!"

"You and your wife..."

"Oh hell no – we're fine – she can take it..." Darien laughed...

"Are you experiencing erectile dysfunction?"

"No..."

"Why are you here then?"

"My wife is in the mood more than I am..."

"How old is she?"

"35..."

"It gets worse as they get older..."

"It does?"

"Oh yea – they want it more in their 40's..."

"Oh – okay..."

"Okay – I told you about CAH – now I'll tell you what low testosterone is – hypogonadism – symptoms include decreased sex drive, erectile dysfunction, inability to conceive, and overall tiredness..."

"How is that treated?"

"That's treated with testosterone replacement therapy – TRT – this is done by injection, a skin patch, or a topical gel – but there are side effects – sleep apnea, acne, blood clot formation, enlarged prostate, and there's also an increased risk of heart attacks and strokes..."

"Damn..."

"Let's wait until your blood test comes back before you start thinking the worst..."

"Too late for that..."

"Mr. Beaufort – how often do you have sex?"

"A couple of times a week..."

"And you've never had a problem getting an erection?"

"Nope..."

"And your wife is satisfied?"

"Very..."

"Focus on that..."

"Okay..."

"I'll call your cell phone with the results..."

"Okay..." Darien said as he got up...

"Have a good day..."

"You too..." Darien said as he left the office...

"You good?" Bazil asked as they got in the car...

"Yea..." Darien sighed...

"I was fucked up when he showed me that speculum too..." Bazil laughed...

"I should fuck you up for letting him do that to me..." Darien laughed...

"Did he tell you about the episiotomy?"

"Hell yea!"

"I'm glad he does it..."

"Why?"

"When I look at my wife, I love her even more..."

"My wife hasn't even had children yet – you have four – I can't wait for Lacey to get pregnant..."

"Really? You want kids?"

"I want at least one..."

"I cried when Beautiee told me she was pregnant – I cried when she gave birth – and the pussy – oh my God..."

"How is it?"

"Well – when she was pregnant – her doctor told me to go home – love my wife – love her pussy – and love our baby..."

"Oh shit! She really told you that?"

"She also told me I was in for a wild ride – she was 12 weeks pregnant – her hormones were on 10 – and she was gonna want ‑ and need my dick..."

"Damn – was she right?"

"Pregnant pussy is the best pussy in the world..."

"Damn – Lacey's pussy is good now – I won't be able to keep up with her when she gets pregnant..." Darien laughed...

"Trust me – that won't be a problem..." Bazil laughed...

"Really?"

"Pregnant pussy is so good – you'll always be ready..."

"Damn!"

"And the best thing about pregnant pussy is this – the pussy stays that way after the baby is born..."

"Yeessss!"

"So how's things with you and Lacey?"

"Good..."

"Good? Why isn't it great?"

"Well... the sex has been great... but..."

"What's wrong?"

"I feel like she's sexing me the way she is because she feels guilty..."

"What's wrong with that?"

"Why didn't she sex me like that before?"

"Why didn't you sex her like that before?"

"Oh so you sayin' it's my fault?"

"Darien – listen to me..."

"Okay..."

"I was having sex with Trevor before I got married – and I continued to have sex with Trevor after we got married..."

"What? You? And Trevor?"

"Yes..."

"So... you're bi-sexual?"

"No..."

"I don't even know what to say..."

"I met Trevor in prison – one thing led to another – I fell for him – I loved him..."

"Oh hell no! Not you man!"

"Yes – me..."

"And Beautiee forgave you?"

"Eventually – but we went through it..."

"I can't believe – I just never thought..."

"I know..."

"How did you get Beautiee to forgive you?"

"I prayed, I cried, I begged..."

"You prayed?"

"Hell yea I prayed – when I died I begged God to give me another chance and please don't let Beautiee live without me..."

"Wait – you died?"

"When I was shot – I died – and Beautiee died – and she came after me..." Bazil said as he started crying...

"Damn man – you got me cryin' n shit!" Darien said as he started crying too...

"After everything I put her through – she came to get me and asked God to let me come back to her..."

"You actually saw God?"

"We actually saw God..."

"Wow – Bazil – I had no idea..."

"Beautiee left me for a week – and she left me for a woman..."

"Oh hell no! A woman? You weren't afraid of losing her?"

"Naa... Sonia couldn't pull Beautiee away from me..." Bazil laughed...

"I hear that!" Darien laughed as they high-fived...

"When Beautiee came back – I punished her for denying me pussy..."

"I punished Lacey..." Darien sighed...

"It was great – wasn't it?"

"It was awesome – and guess what?"

"What?"

"She wants me to punish her again..."

"That's what I'm talkin' about!" Bazil exclaimed as they high-fived...

"Can I ask you something Bazil?"

"Sure – go 'head..."

"Well... as much as I'm enjoying Lacey sexin' me... I keep seeing her sexin' Dexter..."

"Oh I get it – you think she did it with Dexter first..."

"Yea..."

"I thought the same thing when Beautiee slept with Trevor..."

"Wait a min' – you and Beautiee fucked Trevor?"

"Yea..."

"Aww damn!"

"And it fucked me up too – because she enjoyed it..."

"Damn Bazil – I'm sorry..."

"I'm not – she only did that to get revenge – and then she felt like shit..."

"Lacey told me she loves Dexter..." Darien said as he started crying...

"I know that hurts – but le'me ask you a question..."

"Okay..."

"Does she want him?"

"She said she doesn't want him..."

"Do you believe her?"

"I want to – I really do – but I think she's sexin' me the way she is because she's trying to forget him and not because she loves me..."

"Okay – has she been in contact with him?"

"Yes..."

"Aww damn – are you sure?"

"I have her on my account – I have it set up where I can see all her texts..."

"So she still wants him?"

"She told him she doesn't want him..."

"Well that's good..."

"I know... but..."

"You're afraid she's gonna go back to him?"

"Yea..."

"You said you punished her – right?"

"Yea..."

"She enjoyed it – right?"

"Oh yea..."

"And she wants you to do it again – right?"

"Yea..."

"Le'me ask you something..."

"Okay..."

"Why'd you have a threesome with him instead of blowing his fuckin' head off?"

"Because I'm crazy..." Darien sighed...

"Yea – I agree – you're crazy..." Bazil laughed...

"I thought that's what she wanted..." Darien sighed...

"She enjoyed it – didn't she?"

"Yea..."

"So that's why you think she still wants him..."

"Yea..."

"Well – there is one way to get those images out of your head..."

"What's that?"

"Have a threesome with your wife – and another woman..."

"Lacey won't go for that..."

"Beautiee didn't really go for it either – she did it for me..."

"Damn man – your wife really loves you..."

"Yes... she does..."

"What was that like?"

"Every man should experience that at least once in his life..."

"That good huh?"

"Oh yea..."

"How'd you get Beautiee to go for it?"

"Well – the first time was easy – she was already with Sonia for a week so I didn't really have to convince her..." Bazil laughed...

"Wait – the first time? How many times did you do this?"

"Twice..."

"You got her to agree to a threesome twice?"

"The first time we had a threesome – I wound up dead..."

"Bazil – I can't..."

"We invited Sonia – Sonia invited Trevor – Trevor shot me – shot Sonia – Beautiee shot Trevor – she went to jail..."

"Oh my God! What the fuck?"

"I told you – we've been through it..."

"How the hell did you get her to agree to another threesome?"

"We were on our 2nd honeymoon – Beautiee went to the bar, this woman approached her – Beautiee caught me watching them – she brought the woman over and introduced her – we started making out on the dance floor – next thing you know – I'm in bed with the both of them having the time of my life..."

"You are the luckiest mutha fucka I know! How the fuck did you convince Beautiee to do that shit?"

"I followed Beautiee's lead..."

"What do you mean?"

"I let Beautiee take control, I asked permission, she said yes..."

"You asked permission?"

"When we were in bed... I asked may I?"

"Oh shit! So did Beautiee enjoy it?"

"Oh yea..."

"I'd love for Lacey to do that with me..."

"She will..."

"What makes you so sure?"

"She's been talking to Beautiee a lot..."

"Thank God – if anybody can give Lacey advice – Beautiee can..."

"Exactly..."

"I caught her on the phone earlier this morning..."

"You did?"

"She was talking to Beautiee..."

"Oh – okay..."

"She told Beautiee it felt really good..." Darien beamed...

"Man – go home and make love to your wife while you still have privacy!" Bazil laughed...

"Privacy?"

"We have four children – remember?" Bazil said as they both laughed...

"You know this punk mutha fucka had the nerve to ask Lacey when she was leaving me?"

"Oh hell no! He needs to die..."

"Oh he will..." Darien laughed...

"I like that..." Bazil said as he smiled mischievously...

"What?"

"I like the man that's here with me right now..."

"Me too Bazil – me too..."

"So what did Lacey say when he asked when she was leaving you?"

"She told him she's not leaving me..."

"See? I told you!"

"She actually thought I was leaving her when you met me at the bar – I told her I could never leave her – I love her..."

"I know you do..."

"Can I ask you something?"

"Sure – go 'head..."

"Did they both suck your dick at the same time?"

"Bazil didn't answer him – he just started the car.

Chapter 7

"Lacey?"

"I'm in the kitchen..."

"Hey..." Darien breathed as he pulled me into a kiss...

"Hey..."

"I missed you..."

"I missed you too..."

"Come sit in the living room with me – we need to talk..." he said as he took my hand and led me into the living room... "Let's sit down..."

"Okay..." I said as we sat on the couch...

"Lacey – I have something I need to tell you..." he said as he took my hands...

"Okay..."

"When you told me you were lonely – I went to talk to Bazil..."

"I know..."

"You do? How?"

"While you were talking to Bazil I was talking to Beautiee..." I laughed...

"Well..." Darien sighed...

"Darien – what's wrong?"

"Bazil suggested I go get a checkup..."

"Darien it's not your fault.."

"Lacey..." he breathed as he kissed me...
"Stop talking... and listen..."

"Okay..."

"I went for a check-up this morning..."

"So that's why you didn't let me join you in the shower..."

"Yea..."

"What did the doctor say?"

"He had a lot to say..." Darien breathed as he pulled me into a kiss..."

"Like what?"

"He said I should focus..."

"Focus on what?" I asked as he slid my blouse off my shoulders and unclasped my bra...

"He said I should focus..." he started to answer as he slid my bra off and tossed it... "On having sex..."

"Oooohhh..." I breathed as he pushed me down on the couch...

"That's not all..." he said as he opened my pants and slid them off my hips...

"What else did he say?" I breathed as he got up and started to get undressed...

"He said I should also focus..." he breathed as he took off his pants...

"Focus on what?" I breathed...

"On this..." he breathed as he lay down on top of me and thrust himself inside me...

"Ooohhh..." I moaned. I moved my hands down Darien's ' back, grabbed his ass, and pushed him in deeper as he began kissing me and

pushed his tongue in my mouth... "Mmmm...
Mmmm... Mmmm... Mmmm..."

"Mmmph... Mmmph... Mmmph...
Mmmph..." Darien moved my legs up, pinned
them down with his upper body, and fucked me
deeper...

"Mmmm! Mmmm! Mmmm! Mmmm!"

"Mmmph! Mmmph! Mmmph! Mmmph!"
Darien pushed himself up on his hands and
began pounding my pussy...

"Darien... Yeess.... Fuck me... I'm
cumming!"

"Uggh! Uggh! Uggh! Uggh! Uuuggghhh!"
Darien collapsed on top of me and started kissing
me again... "I love you Lacey..."

"I love you too..." Darien got up and began
kissing me down my stomach... "Darien..." I
whispered. When I saw Darien's head between
my legs, I thought he was going to devour me
right away but he had other ideas... "Darien...
what are you doing?"

"Be still..." he answered. I had no idea
what Darien was doing. He pushed my legs apart
and held them apart with his hands and all I
could see was his head...

"You..." he breathed as he kissed my
thigh... "Are..." he breathed as he kissed my thigh
a little further...

"So..." he breathed as he kissed my inner
thigh... "Beautiful..." he breathed and then he

pulled my body to his mouth and began devouring me...

"DARIEN!" I moaned as I grabbed his head. Darien didn't let up and I didn't want him to... "Haah... Haah... Haah... Haah... HHHAAAAAAHHH!" I arched my back, came up off the couch, and fell back down. Darien came up from in between my legs, lay down on top of me, and thrust himself inside me again... "Darien..."

"I want you to have my baby Lacey..." he breathed and then he began kissing me again...

"Mmmm... Mmmm... Mmmm... Mmmm..."

"Mmmph... Mmmph... Mmmph... Mmmph..."

"Beautiee..." Bazil called out...

"I'm in the library..."

"Hey..."

"Hey..."

"Come upstairs with me..." he said as he held out his hand for Beautiee to take...

"Okay..." she sighed as she turned off her computer, got up from her desk, and took Bazil's hand. Bazil led Beautiee upstairs and into the bedroom. When he got her inside, he closed the door, pushed her against it, and kissed her hard... "Mmmm...." she moaned...

"Thank you..."

"You're welcome..."

"I love you so much..."

"I love you too..."

"How much time do we have before the kids get home?" he breathed as he undressed her...

"Two hours..."

'How long before Lydia wakes up?"

"I just put her down for a nap before you came in..." Beautiee answered as Bazil took her by the hand and led her to the bed...

"Was she full before she went to sleep?" Bazil asked as Beautiee helped him get undressed...

"Yes..."

"Good – that gives us some time..." he breathed as he pushed Beautiee down onto the bed. Beautiee spread her legs and her arms as Bazil got on the bed and lay on top of her... "What was that you whispered to me this morning?" he asked as he thrust himself inside her...

"Bazil..." she moaned...

"Yes Beautiee..."

"Please..." she moaned...

"Please what?" he growled as he began pounding her pussy..."

"Please... Fuck me..."

"As you wish..." he growled as he put her legs up on his shoulders and continued pounding her pussy...

"Haah... Haah... Haah... Haah..."

"Uuugh... Uuugh... Uuugh... Uuugh..."

"Haah... Haah... Haah... Haah...

"Uuugh... Uuugh... Uuugh... Uuugh..."

"Fuck... Bazil... I'm cumming..."

"I'm cumming with you..."

"Aaagh! Aaagh! Aaagh! Aaagh! AAAGGGHHH!"

Uggh! Uggh! Uggh! Uggh! UUUGGGHHH!"

"Remind me to do it again..." Beautiee panted...

"Do what?"

"Whatever I did to make you fuck me like that..." she breathed as she pulled him into a kiss...

"You said please..." Bazil breathed as he kissed her...

"Ooohhh... that's right... you like that..."

"I love it..." he breathed as he kissed her again..."

"So do I..." she breathed as they continued kissing...

"I love you so much..." I breathed...

"I love you too..."

"I can't wait to have our baby..."

"You mean it?"

"Yes Darien – I mean it – we're gonna have a baby..."

"Let's go celebrate – I'll take you anywhere you want to go..."

"Okay!" I squealed as I jumped up...

"Where are you going?" Darien laughed...

"I'm going in the shower – and then I'm getting dressed – and then I'm going out to dinner – with you!" I squealed as I threw my arms around his neck...

"I'm coming with you..." he breathed as he kissed me...

"Okay..." I breathed as I took his hand and led him to the Master Bathroom...

"Let me see... which one do I like... I have so many to choose from.. ooohhh... I think I'll start with this one..." Dexter said as he sent Lacey the video. After he sent her the video, he text her the following message... "Just wanted to let you know I'm thinking about you... talk to you soon... have a great day..." After he sent the text message he called her... "Hmmm... voicemail..."

"This is Lacey – you know what to do..."

"Yes Lacey... this is Dexter... and you're right... I know exactly what do do..."

Chapter 8

"DARIEN! I'M CUMMING! AAAGGGHHH!"

"UUUGGGHHH!"

"Darien..." I panted...

"Yes Lacey..." he breathed as he kissed me...

"I'm weak..."

"Let's get dressed – I need to feed you..."

"Okay..." I breathed as he picked me up in his arms and led me into the bedroom. After we got dressed, Darien took me by the hand and pulled me out the bedroom towards the living room...

"Darien... wait..."

"What's wrong?"

"My phone..."

"Leave it..."

"Okay..." I sighed as he pulled me into the living room towards the front door...

"You ready?" he asked...

"I'm ready..." Darien pulled me into a kiss and held me for a few minutes. I didn't move. I barely breathed. It felt so good to be held by him, loved by him...

"Let's go..." I didn't ask where we were going. I didn't care. I looked over at him and he was happy...

"We're here..."

"Ooohhh... bin100 – oh Darien – thank you!"

"You're welcome..." he said as he opened the door, jumped out the car, and hurried around to my side to open the door for me. After he opened the door for me he picked me up in his arms and put me down...

"Darien – I love you..."

"I love you too – let's go inside..." he said as he took me by the hand and pulled me towards the entrance...

"Welcome to bin100 – do you have a reservation?" the hostess asked...

"Yes we do..."

"May I have your name?"

"Beaufort..."

"Mr. & Mrs. Beaufort – come with me..." she said as she took us to our table and we sat down...

"Your waiter will be with you in a moment – I'll be right back with some garlic bread – would you like to sample our wine?"

"Yes please!" I squealed...

"Easy Lacey – you haven't had anything to eat yet..." Darien laughed...

"I'll be right back..." she said as she left...

"I love this place..." I sighed...

"I know..."

"Here you are..." the hostess said as she placed the garlic bread on the table..."

"Ooohhh... this is good..." I breathed as I took a bite...

"Today's wine is 207 Pinot Noir King Estate – Willamette Valley 2015..." she said as she poured two small glasses...

"Ooohhh – this is good..." I breathed...

"It is good..." Darien agreed...

"I'm glad you like it – if you'd like to add it to your meal, please let the waiter know..." she said as she walked away...

"Good afternoon – my name is Stewart – I'll be your server – would you like to see a menu or do you know what you're having?"

"I know what we're having..." Darien answered...

"Will you be adding today's wine to your meal?"

"Yes we will..."

"Okay – what will you be having today?"

"We'll have the Four Course PrixFixe Dinner..."

"Okay – may I have your first course?"

"Fried Calamari..." I answered...

"Angus Meatballs..." Darien answered...

"Your second course will be the House Salad with Vinaigrette – may I have your third course?"

"I'll have the Penne Bolognese..." I answered...

"I'll have the Ziti Genovese..." Darien answered...

"May I have your dessert?"

"Oh noo..." I laughed...

"I meant to ask for your order..." Steward laughed...

"I know – I'll have the New York Style Cheesecake with Strawberry Puree..."

"I'll have the German Chocolate Cake..." Darien said...

"Okay – I'll be back with your wine..." Steward said as he walked away to place our order...

"Well isn't this nice?" Dexter said as he came over to our table...

"Come Dexter – sit!" Darien said as he moved over and my heart sank in my chest...

"Thank you for inviting me to sit – I was just going to ask Lacey if she got my message..."

"She didn't get your message – but I did – and now I have a message for you..." Darien growled as he moved his hand under the table. Once I saw the expression change on Dexter's face I knew what Darien was doing... "Do you feel that?"

"Yea..." Dexter answered...

"How 'bout this?"

"Uugghh... yea..."

"Listen to me mutha fucka – stay the fuck away from my wife – don't text her – don't call her – leave her the fuck alone – or I'll rip your got damn balls off and force you to choke on them – am I clear?"

"Perfectly..." Dexter gritted through clenched teeth..."

"Good – not get the fuck outta here!" Dexter got up from the table and left the restaurant without saying a word.

Chapter 9

We ate without speaking. When we got home, Darien opened the door and stepped aside so I could go in first. When I turned to see if Darien was coming inside, I realized he wasn't... "Where are you going?"

"I'll be back later..." he answered as he went back to the car, got in, and sped off...

"I might as well check my messages..." I sighed as I went into the bedroom to check my phone...

"Lacey – I tried. I never intended to fall in love with you – but now that I have, I can't let you go. We're meant to be together and I'll stop at nothing to have you. Oh – by the way – your husband just cost you $2,000 – bring it to me when you come see me tonight at the Holiday Inn – if I don't see you – your husband will get a nice gift from me – a copy of the video I sent you earlier. Love, Dexter"

"Oh my God..." I whispered as I started crying and continued reading his messages...

"Just wanted to let you know I'm thinking about you... talk to you soon... have a great day..."

"Oh God... please... no..." I cried as I watched the video. I checked my messages and played the message he left for me...

"Yes Lacey... this is Dexter... and you're right... I know exactly what do do..."

"Lacey..." Dexter breathed...

"I can't make it tonight..."

"If you don't come see me... you leave me no choice..."

"No... please... I can come now if you want..."

"That's what I want to hear..."

"I'll bring you the money – I promise – I'll do whatever you want – please don't send that video to my husband..."

"I'll see you soon..."

"Shit – Fuck – I gotta think! I'll get an Uber – that's it – I'll get an Uber to the bank – I'll withdraw the money – I'll go to the hotel – I'll meet him in the lobby – I'll give him the money – and then I'll leave..." I said out loud as I hurried out the door...

"Darien! What brings you here?" Bazil asked. Darien didn't answer – he just broke down crying. Bazil got up, went over to the door, locked it, and pulled Darien into a hug... "What happened?"

"We made love..."

"Okay..."

"It was good..."

"Sit down..."

"You got anything to drink?"

"Yea – I got something – hang on..." Bazil said as he pulled a bottle of Hennessey from his desk drawer, took out a glass, and poured Darien a drink...

"Thank you..." he breathed and then he gulped it down..."

"You made love?"

"Yea..."

"It was good?"

"Yea..."

"Why are you here?"

"I told her I went to the doctor..."

"Ohh..."

"I told her the doctor said I should focus on having sex..."

"Okay..."

"We made love..."

"Okay..."

"I told her I want her to have my baby..."

"Really? What'd she say?"

"She said yes..."

"Congratulations!"

"I told her I was taking her out to celebrate..."

"Okay!" Bazil beamed...

"We went to bin100..."

"Nice!"

"Dexter comes over o our table..."

"Oh shit!"

"I invited him to sit down..."

"Why the fuck would you do that?"

"Mutha fucka goin' say thanks for the invite – I was just going to ask Lacey if she got my message!"

"What the fuck!"

"I put my hands in his pants – I grabbed his balls – I squeezed – and I said she didn't get your message – but I did – and now I have a message for you – do you feel that?"

"Oh shit!" Bazil exclaimed as they high-fived...

"I said listen to me mutha fucka – stay the fuck away from my wife – don't text her – don't call her – leave her the fuck alone – or I'll rip your got damn balls off and force you to choke on them – am I clear?"

"Yo!" Bazil laughed... "Darien – my man – I didn't know you had that in you! Was he clear?"

"Perfectly..." Darien answered through gritted teeth imitating Dexter..."

"Aaaah Haaaahhh!" Bazil laughed...

"Bazil – you don't understand..."

"What?"

"I can't look at her right now – it was all I could do to sit there and eat – I want to choke the life out of her right now!" Darien gritted..."

"DARIEN!"

"I'm sorry..." he said as he fell back on the couch and started crying...

"DARIEN! LOOK AT ME!"

"WHAT?!"

"I need you to listen to me..."

"Fuck you – I'ma go..."

"Is that what you really wanna do?"

"No..." he sighed as he sat back down...

"Aiight then – come over here – you said you have access to Lacey's phone – right?"

"Yes..." Darien answered as he got up and sat down at Bazil's desk...

"Okay – I need you to log in – pull up the account – and let's see what's going on..."

"After we made love... we went in the shower... we made love again... we got dressed – Lacey wanted to bring her phone but I told her to leave it..." Darien explained as he logged in...

"So she never got the message..."

"What?"

"You said you told her to leave her phone – she never got the message..."

"Oh shit!"

"Pull up the account – let's see what's going on..."

"Okay..." Darien acknowledged as he pulled up the account and they both started reading...

"Just wanted to let you know I'm thinking about you... talk to you soon... have a great day..."

"Mutha Fucka!" Darien exclaimed as he pounded his fist on the desk...

"Damn..." Bazil sighed as the video popped up and Darien started watching...

"Stop it..." Bazil said...

"Hell no! I need to see this shit!"

"No... you don't need to see that man..." Bazil said as he took the mouse and stopped the video from playing. Darien saw there was a message from him and played it...

"Yes Lacey... this is Dexter... and you're right... I know exactly what do do..."

"He's got balls!" Bazil exclaimed...

"Not for long..." Darien said as he read the latest text message...

"Oh my God -he's blackmailing her!"

"What?"

"She's on her way to meet him at the Holiday Inn..."

"Le'me see that!" Bazil exclaimed as he started reading the conversation...

"Lacey – I tried. I never intended to fall in love with you – but now that I have, I can't let you go. We're meant to be together and I'll stop at nothing to have you. Oh – by the way – your husband just cost you $2,000 – bring it to me when you come see me tonight at the Holiday Inn – if I don't see you – your husband will get a nice gift from me – a copy of the video I sent you earlier. Love, Dexter"

"I'll fuckin' kill him!" Darien exclaimed as he got up to leave...

"Darien- wait!"

"Fuck you! I'm out!" Bazil jumped up from behind the desk and grabbed Darien into a bear hug... "Let go of me!"

"Not until you listen to me!"

"Fine – I'll listen!"

"I'ma let you go – but..."

"I'll listen!"

"Okay – first – I need you to go save everything in the account before she deletes it..."

"What the fuck is that supposed to do?"

"Dammit Darien – just do it!"

"Fine!" Darien snapped as he went back over to the computer and saved all the texts and video... "Okay – I saved it – now what?"

"Now I want you to look at her Uber trips..."

"I'm looking..."

"Did she leave for the hotel?"

"Yea – she just left – I can still catch her..."

"You need to let her give him the money..."

"What? Are you crazy?"

"You need to let her give him the money..."

"Why? Why the fuck should I do that?"

"Because – once you have him arrested – he can be charged with extortion..."

"What the fuck are you talking about?"

"Right now he feels he has the upper hand – that's why he over-stepped..."

"So?"

"So – now you have proof that he's been stalking your wife and also blackmailing your wife..."

"I don't want him in jail – I want him dead!" Darien exclaimed as he banged his fist on the desk...

"He'll be dead – trust me..."

"Bazil – what are you saying?"

"I'm saying let's go meet your wife at the Holiday Inn..." Bazil answered as he got up...

"That's what I'm talkin' about..." Darien said as they left...

"There she is..." Darien said as they watched her walking into the hotel...

"Remember what I said..." Bazil said...

"I know – I need to let her give him the money!"

"I'm going back to my car..." Bazil said as he walked away from Darien...

"Hello Lacey..." Dexter beamed when he saw her...

"Let's get this over with..." Lacey snapped...

"I got us a room..."

"I never said I was sleeping with you..."

"Listen Bitch!" he gritted through his teeth as he grabbed her arm... "I'm done playing with you – you're going to come to my room..." he breathed as he pulled her into a kiss... "Give me my money..." he breathed as he kissed her again... "And give me some pussy..."

"Please Dexter... don't make me do this..."

"I won't make you – but if you don't – I'll send the video to your husband..."

"You said if I pay you..."

"Yes... I did..."

"Let's go to the bar... I need a drink..."

"I have alcohol in the room... I'll give you a drink..."

"I'd rather go to the bar..."

"Okay... we can go to the bar... and after you have your drink... I can hit send on this video..."

"No... please... I just need a drink... then I'll give you your money... and I'll go to the room with you..."

"Okay – let's go get your drink..." Dexter said as he put his arm around me and walked me over to the bar...

"Hi – what can I get you?" the bartender asked...

"Two shots of Hennessey..." Dexter answered...

"Two shots of Hennessey – coming right up..." the bartender said as he poured the shots... "Here you go..."

"Thank you – Lacey – pay the man..."

"Okay..." I said as I took the envelope out my purse with cash in it, laid it down on the bar, and pushed it over to Dexter...

"Thank you..." Dexter said, smiling at me mischievously...

"Lacey!" Darien called out and then he started walking towards us...

"Oh my God..." I whispered...

"There you are..." Darien said as he pulled me into a kiss...

"Darien – I..."

"You're ready to go home – c'mon – let's go..." he said as he put his arm around me and helped me down off the bar stool. I walked out the bar, through the lobby, and out the hotel to the parking lot without saying a word. When we got to the car, Darien pulled me into a kiss and I started to cry... "Don't cry Lacey..." he breathed as he kissed my eyes and my tears...

"Darien – I..."

"Ssshhh..." he breathed as he kissed me again... "Let's go home..." he said as he opened the door for me...

"Okay..." I sighed as I got in and sat down. Darien got in the car, started the car, and took my hand in his as we rode. I wasn't sure what was happening but I was happy. When we got home, Darien opened the door for me and waited for me to go inside. I went inside and this time when I turned around – Darien was coming in behind me... "Darien... I'm sorry..."

"Let's go sit down..." he said as he took me by the hand and led me into the living room.

After we sat down, Darien spoke... "When I left earlier this afternoon – I was angry – I was so angry I wanted to hurt you..."

"I'm sorry..." I whispered as I started crying...

"When Dexter came to the table, he said he was going to ask if you received his message – so I thought you received his message and didn't tell me..."

"I didn't get his message earlier – I swear..."

"I know you didn't..."

"You know? How?"

"I went to see Bazil..."

"You did?"

"Yes..."

"Okay..."

"Bazil suggested I log into the account and retrieve the messages..."

"Oh my God!" I cried...

"Bazil reminded me that you didn't get the message because you left your phone at home..."

"Did you see the video?"

"Yes..."

"Oh God... I'm sorry!" I cried. Darien took me in his arms and held me...

"Lacey – listen to me..."

"But Darien..."

"Listen to me..."

"Okay..."

"I know he blackmailed you..."

"I gave him $2,000..."

"It's okay..."

"He was trying to force me to sleep with him – he said if I didn't – he'd send you the video..."

"Lacey – I'm glad you gave him the money..."

"Why would you be glad I gave him the money after you saw the video?"

"I needed him to take the money so he can be charged with extortion..."

"How long have you been monitoring my phone?"

"Long enough to confirm you were cheating on me..."

"I'm sorry..."

"I know..."

"If he contacts you again – I want you to tell me..."

"How much longer am I going to have to do this?"

"I took you out the hotel – he's pissed – he'll contact you again – it won't be long now...

"That's my phone..." I said as I took it out my pocket, looked at it, and read the following text...

"I told you I wasn't playing with you – you didn't do what you promised – now you have to pay – and this time – your husband won't be able to save you..."

Darien – here..." I said as I handed him my phone...

"Gotcha!" Darien said as he smiled.

Chapter 10

"Good morning..." I yawned... "Darien? Darien – where are you? Hmmm – maybe he's in the kitchen..." I said as I got up out of bed...

"Darien? Where is he?" I asked as I went into the living room...

"Good morning..." he said as he came in...

"Good morning – where were you?"

"Come in the kitchen..." I got up and followed him into the kitchen and sat at the table...

"Here..." he said as he put the grand carmel macchiato in front of me...

"You went to Starbucks!"

"Yea..." he said as he took the other stuff out the bag...

"What's that?"

"This is a security system..."

"Oh wow..."

"I'm going to get this up – and then I'll show you how it works..."

"We live in an apartment – it's pretty hard to get through that door..."

"Lacey – come with me..." he said as he got up from the table, took me by the hand, and pulled me towards the door... "I'm going to go outside this door – and no matter what I say – don't open this door..." he said as he left and closed the door... "Open the door..."

"No..." I laughed...

"I said open the door..."

"No..." I laughed again...

"You won't open the door – okay – have it your way..." Darien said as he went downstairs...

"Darien..." I said as I opened the door... "Come back upstairs..." I laughed...

"AAAAGGGHHHH!" Darien exclaimed as he charged up the stairs, grabbed me, and pushed me inside... "Now... do you see how easy it was for me to get in here?"

"The only reason you got in here was because..."

"Go ahead – say it..."

"Because I opened the door..."

"Exactly..."

"Okay – you made your point..." I sighed...

"Good – now I'm going to put a camera in the door – right up here..."

"You can see it..."

"So what?"

"Okay..."

"I'm also going to put a camera in the living room and the kitchen..."

"Okay..."

"This is a motion detector..." he said as he took it out the box...

"Looks like a camera..."

"It's not – it's a motion detector – once we set the alarm – anybody that comes through that door will trigger the motion detector..."

"How will you know when it's been triggered?"

"You'll get a notification on your cell – it will say new video – you open the app – you watch the video..."

"That's it?"

"That's it..." he answered as he continued setting up...

"Do you really think he's going to come here?"

"Yes..." he answered as he stood on the step-ladder and put up the motion detector...

"I don't even want to leave the house now..."

"You can leave the house – you'll just leave with me..."

"I can take an Uber..."

"You took an Uber yesterday – look how that turned out..."

"I'm sorry..."

"That wasn't your fault..."

"Yes it was – this is all my fault!" Darien came over to me and pulled me into a kiss...

"Okay..." I sighed...

"Okay what?"

"I'll stop talking..."

"Go into your apps and download Simply Safe..."

"Okay..." Darien watched as I downloaded the app and then he took my phone...

"What are you doing?"

"I'm logging you into the account..."

"What's the email?"

"Mine..."

"What's the password?"

"I'm not telling you..."

"Why?"

"If you're in a situation where you lose your phone or somebody hacks your phone and tries to log in – I'll get a notification that someone tried to access the account..."

"Ooohhh..."

"I'm going to log you in myself..."

"Okay..." I watched Darien log me in and then he gave the phone back to me... "Okay – the options are off, home, and away..."

"I see..."

"You see how it goes from camera to camera?"

"I see..."

"Now – I want you to push home..."

"Okay..." I said as I pushed the button...

"Now – come with me..." he said as he took me by the hand and walked me towards the front door...

"What are you doing?"

"What's it feel like I'm doing?" he asked as he came up behind me and began kissing me on my neck...

"Ooohh... it feels like..."

"Tell me..."

"It feels like you want to make love to me..."

"Come with me..." he breathed as he picked me up and carried me into the bedroom...

"Are there any cameras in here?" I asked as he lay me down on the bed and then he lay down on top of me...

"Do you want a camera in here?" he breathed as he kissed me...

"Yeesss..."

"We can do that..." he breathed as he kissed me again. Darien continued kissing me as he ran his hand over my breasts, down my stomach, and between my legs...

"Darien..." I moaned... "Yes Lacey..." he breathed as he spread my legs and eased himself inside me...

"Darien..."

"Lacey..." he breathed and then he pushed his tongue in my mouth and began thrusting harder...

"Mmmm... Mmmm... Mmmm... Mmmm..."

"Mmmph... Mmmph... Mmmph... Mmmph..." I moved my hands down Darien's back, grabbed his ass, and dug my nails into his ass as I pushed him in deeper...

"Mmmm... Mmmm... Mmmm... Mmmm..."

"Mmmph... Mmmph... Mmmph... Mmmph..." Darien moved my legs up, held them in place by my thighs, and began pounding my pussy... "MMMM... MMMM... MMMM... MMMM..."

"MMMPH... MMMPH... MMMPH... MMMPH..." Darien's body was tensing up, his legs began to tremble, and he pushed my legs up a bit more, lifting my ass up off the bed as he pounded my spot... and I started screaming...

"DAARRIIIEEENN! I'M CUMMING! AAHH! AAHH! AAHH! AAHH! AAAHHH!"

"UUGGHH! UUGGHH! UUGGHH! UUGGHH! UUUGGGHHH!"

"Shit!" I panted as Darien fell down on top of me...

"I love you Lacey..." he breathed as he kissed me...

"I love you too..."

"We're going to need a bigger place..."

"We are?"

"We can't have the baby in here with us..."

"He can sleep in here for a little while..."

"No..." Darien breathed as he kissed me again... "He can't..."

"Why not?"

"Because you make too much noise..." he laughed...

"Me? What about you?"

"That's your pussy's fault..." he said as he bust out laughing... "Shit – that's my phone..."

"Don't get it..."

"I have to..." he breathed as he reached over me and grabbed the phone...

"Hello?"

"Mr. Beaufort – it's Dr. Har – did I catch you at a bad time?"

"No doctor – I can talk..." Darien said as he sat up...

"Listen – I need you to come to see me as soon as possible..."

"Is this about my tests results?"

"Mr. Beaufort?"

"Yes doctor?"

"I need you to come see me..."

"Okay – I'll come today..."

"How's 12 o'clock?"

"I'll be there at 12..." Darien said and then he hung up...

"You want me to go with you?"

"No..."

"Are you okay?"

"I'm fine – we haven't eaten – let's take a shower, get dressed, and I'll make breakfast..." he said as he got up...

"Okay..." I sighed as I got up. We went in the shower, came out, dried off, and went back in the bedroom as if we didn't just get finished making love... "Darien..."

"Yes Lacey?"

"Talk to me..."

"I'm okay..."

"No..." I said as I got up and went over to him... "You're not..."

"Lacey..." he breathed as he pulled me into a hug...

"Yes Darien?"

"I'm okay – I'm just wondering why he wouldn't tell me my results over the phone..."

"My gynecologist does the same thing..." I sighed...

"She does?"

"I go see her – I get a checkup – she tells me if you don't hear from me that means everything's fine – then she calls me to tell me everything's fine..." I laughed...

"What if everything's not fine Lacey?"

"Everything's fine..." I breathed as I kissed him...

"Lacey..."

"Everything's fine..." I breathed as I kissed him again...

"Lacey..."

"Everything's fine..." I breathed as I kissed him again...

"Everything's fine..." he breathed as he kissed me...

"That's better..." I breathed...

"C'mon – I'll make you breakfast..." he said as he took me by the hand and we went into the kitchen...

"And now... I'll sit... and I'll wait..." Dexter said as he pulled up in front of their building...
"What video should I send today... ooohhh... I like this one...." he said as he pulled his dick out and started stroking it...

That's was delicious..." I said...
"You're welcome..." Darien said as he got up and took the dishes off the table...
"You sure you don't want me to go with you?" I asked as I went behind him and held him. Darien turned around and pulled me to him...
"Lacey – I want to go by myself..."
"Okay – we can pick up where we left off after the doctor gives you the good news..."
"That sounds good..." Darien breathed as he pulled me into a kiss.

Chapter 11

"Dexter... yes... don't stop..."

"I won't Lacey... Uuuggghhh..." Dexter was jerking his dick rapidly as he continued watching the video...

"Dexter..." Haah... I'm cumming..."

"I'm cumming with you Lacey..."

"Aaaahhhh!"

"Uuuuggghh!"

"Uh uh – no the fuck you not – you nasty mutha fucka – we got kids over here – that's it – I'm calling the police!" the grandmother snapped as she banged on the window. Dexter started the car and sped off... "Nasty mutha fucka – I bet' not eva catch your ass 'round here again!" she exclaimed as she was waiving her hands...

"Is there a problem Maam?" Sergeant Hurley asked as he pulled up...

"Hell yea there's a fuckin' problem!"

"Maam – I need you to calm down..."

"I'm sorry officer – he just made me so got damn mad..."

"Let me get out and talk to you a minute..." Sergeant Hurley said as he got out the car and came over to her...

"I wish you were here a few minutes earlier..."

"What happened Maam?"

"He was jerkin' off in his car!"

"What?" Sergeant Hurley asked as he started taking notes...

"He was parked right here where you parked – I had just come back from taking my grandchi'ren to school – I put them on the bus 'round the corner..."

"Is that when you saw him?"

"So I came 'round the corner – I'm 'bout ready to go back in my house – and he's jerkin' his dick watching some video on his phone!"

"Right here? In broad daylight?"

"Yes!! Nasty mutha fucka – I banged on the window!"

"Did you get a look at anything besides..."

"His nasty dick?"

"Yea..." Sergeant Hurley laughed...

"He was black – my complexion..."

"Was he tall?"

"I think so – his head almost touched the hood..."

"Anything else you can tell me?"

"He was driving a Black Lincoln Continental..."

"You sure?"

"Oh yea – my husband had one a dem..."

"What's your name Maam?"

"My name Alice..."

"Thank you Alice – here's my card – if you see anything else – you call me – okay?"

"Okay Jeremy..." Alice beamed...

"You have a nice day..."

"You too Jeremy..." she beamed as she went up into her building...

"Stupid Bitch – now I gotta wait around the corner – oh well – as long as she doesn't come back downstairs..." Dexter said as he parked the car, got out, closed the door, and walked towards the building...

"I'm going to leave now..."

"Hurry back..."

"I will – I promise..." Darien breathed as he kissed me... "I want you to arm the house as soon as I leave – I'm going to check my phone to make sure you did it right..."

"Okay..."

"I love you – I'll see you later..." he said as he hurried out the door...

"Hmmm... since he's going to check his phone... maybe I'll give him something to look at..." I said as I went towards the living room...

"There he is..." Dexter gritted. Dexter waited for Darien to get in the car and take off before he went into the building and started up the stairs...

"Home..." I said out loud as I set the alarm... "This is for you Darien..." I said as I began unbuttoning my blouse...

"Knock... knock... knock..."
"Who the hell is that? Oh shoot – I can look on the camera..." I said as I picked up my phone... "Oh my God..."
"Lacey..." Dexter called out...
"Get the fuck outta here Dexter!" I yelled...
"Lacey... if you let me in... I promise... I won't hurt you... I just wanna talk..."
"Fuck you!"
"I'd really like that..."
"You're being recorded mutha fucka!" I screamed...
"On what – oh – I see – you have a camera – I mean – you had a camera..." he said as he pointed the gun at the camera and shot it...
"Oh my God! Just leave!" I yelled...

"Hello Mr. Beaufort – go on in – the doctor will see you now..."
"Okay – thank you..." Darien said as he went down the hall and walked in Dr. Har's office...
"Hello Mr. Beaufort..."
"Just tell me..." Darien sighed...

"Everything's fine..."

"Did you say everything's fine?"

"Everything's fine..."

"Oh thank God..."

"I wanted to talk you because something brought you to see me..."

"Yes – my wife..."

"That's not all that's going on..."

"You're right..."

"As men – we put a lot of pressure on ourselves – especially when it comes to sex..."

"What do you mean?"

"We want to satisfy our ladies – but we're so worried about making sure they're satisfied we forget we need to be satisfied too..."

"Exactly..."

"I know you love your wife – I know you want your wife – but I also think you want to relax at the end of the day because you're under a lot of pressure at work – but you don't want to tell your wife that – so you have a couple of drinks after dinner – a few too many..."

"Yea..."

"Are you still drinking?"

"Yes – but I don't have as many as I used to..."

"Well that's good..."

"I told my wife what you said..."

"I said a lot..." Dr. Har laughed...

"You said I should focus on sex..."

"Pretty much..."

"I've been focusing on that a lot..." Darien said as he smiled...

"Good for you..."

"Thank you doctor..."

"There's one more thing..."

"What's that?"

"Your testosterone is within normal range – but... well..."

"Just say it..."

"You're at nearly 1,000 – I'm surprised that with your age and with your sex drive you haven't worn your wife out!" he laughed...

"Really?"

"I'm serious!"

"Oh wow – well – I don't have any plans to let up soon – we're working on a baby..."

"Congratulations..."

"Thank you..."

"I want you to come see me in six months..."

"Why?"

"I want to do some blood work and see if your levels go any higher..."

"Okay – but you said everything's fine – right?"

"Yes Darien..." Dr. Har laughed... "Everything's fine..."

"Thank you..."

"You're welcome – now go on – go work on that baby!"

"I will doctor – thank you!" Darien yelled as he ran down the hall...

"Lacey... check your phone..."

"Oh God!" I exclaimed as I checked my phone and saw another video... "Why are you doing this to me?" I cried...

"Open the door Lacey..."

"No!"

"Do you want me to send your husband the video?"

"No... please... don't..." I cried...

"Open the door for me... and I'll delete it..."

"No..."

"I'm sorry Lacey... I tried to be nice to you... your husband's going to love this one..."

"No – I'll open the door!" I exclaimed as I ran and snatched the door open...

"I see you started without me..." he breathed as he pulled me into a kiss and finished unbuttoning my shirt...

"No... please..."

"You don't want me?"

"No... I just want my husband..."

"Are you sure you don't want me? After all – there was no forcible entry... you let me in..."

"You promised to delete the video..."

"I'm a man of my word..." Dexter said as he held up his phone and showed me a list of videos... "Now... let's see... which one was that..." he said as scrolled through all the videos...

"You're a monster!" I screamed...

"Aaahhh – here it is – oh shoot – I think I may have hit send my mistake...

"AAAAGGGHHH!" I screamed as I lunged for him and he caught me...

"You feel so good in my arms... yes... fight me..."

"Let go of me!"

"Okay – I'll let go of you... and I'll disable this camera too..." he said as he pointed the gun and shot the camera...

"You won't get away with this..."

"Actually – I will – you let me in – we've been having an affair – you told me you were leaving your husband – I have the proof in my phone..."

"Give me that!" I said as I tried to snatch it away from him, tripped, and wound up falling into his arms...

"See? You want me just as much as I want you..." he breathed as he wrapped his arm around my neck and began choking me..."

"Please... I can't breathe..."

"Come with me..." he gritted as he pulled me into the living room...

"Let's sit down..." I said, deliberately trying to direct his attention away from the camera..."

"Okay – we'll sit – and you're going to write!" he said as he pulled out a pad and a pen...

"What?"

"You're going to write Darien a letter..."

"Okay..."

"You're going to tell him you're leaving him to be with me..."

"Okay..."

"If you try anything..." he said as he moved closer to me..." I'll kill you..."

"I won't try anything... I promise..."

"I can't trust you..."

"You can trust me... I'll prove it..."

"Prove it..." I picked up the pen and wrote Darien the following...

"Dear Darien, I love you with all my heart but I love Dexter too. I've tried to fight my feelings for him but I can't. It isn't fair to either one of you – so I've decided to follow my heart and go be with Dexter. Lacey..."

"Let me see..." he said as he picked up the letter and read it... "I guess I can trust you – I'm still not convinced though..." he breathed as he pushed me down on the couch and lay on top of me...

"Dexter... we can't..."

"See – I knew it..."

"I... I wanna leave before Darien gets back – I don't want him to catch us – like the last time..."

"Hmmm – you have a point – get up – c'mon – let's go..."

"Sergeant Hurley..."

"Jeremy – this Alice!"

"What's wrong?"

"That car I told you about – it's 'round the corner – I seen it when I went to get me some cigarettes..."

"I'll come by and check it out..."

"Thank you Jeremy..." she said as she hung up...

"Sarge?"

"Yea Ed?"

"We got a report of shots fired at 659 West Avenue..."

"I'm on my way over there now – some perv was spotted jerking off in his car earlier this morning..." Sergeant Hurley said as he hurried out...

"I can't wait to get home to Lacey..." Darien sighed as he got in the car... "Le'me see if she set the alarm... ooohhh... what's this?" he beamed as he watched me unbuttoning my shirt... "Oh hell no!" he exclaimed as he saw Dexter... "Oh shit – he's got a gun – Laacceey!" he exclaimed as he hurried out the parking lot. Darien was speeding twice the speed limit when the officer pulled him over...

"License and registration..."

"Officer please – my wife – he's got a gun!"

"Who's got a gun?"

"Please – he's going to kill her!"

"What's your address?"

"659 West Avenue..."

"Wait here..."

"Sergeant Hurley..."

"Sarge – I just pulled over a Darien Beaufort – he claims someone has a gun on his wife...

"I'm on my way to follow up on a complaint of shot's fired – what's his address?"

"659 West Avenue..."

"Oh shit – that's where I'm headed – meet me there..."

"Okay Sarge..." the officer said as he hurried over to the car...

"There's been a report of shots fired at your address – follow me!" the officer exclaimed and then he hurried to his car and sped off...

"Hey Darien..." Bazil answered...

"He's got a gun!"

"Dexter?"

"Yes!"

"Did you call the police?"

"They're on their way!"

"So am I!" Bazil said as he hung up and ran out the door.

Chapter 12

Sergeant Hurley was the first to arrive...
"Jeremy – the car's over there..." Alice said...

"Get in your house – and stay there!"
Sergeant Hurley said as he drew his gun...

"Officer – what's going on?" Alice asked as
the officer that pulled Darien over got out the car,
followed by Darien...

"Get back!"

"That's my wife!"

"We got it! Now get back!" he yelled again
as Bazil pulled up and jumped out his car...

"Darien!"

"Bazil – they won't let me go!"

"They got it..." Bazil said as he pulled
Darien into a hug...

"That's my wife man..." Darien cried...

"I know, I know..." Bazil said...

"Police! Open the door!" I ran to the door
but Dexter caught me...

"You fuckin' called the police? I knew I
couldn't trust you!" he yelled as he hit me upside
my head with the butt of the gun...

"Aaaggghhh!"

"Open the fuckin' door!" Sergeant Hurley yelled...

"You come in here and she's dead!"

"You don't wanna do that..."

"I won't let her leave..."

"You don't have any other options..."

"I'll kill her – and then I'll kill myself!"

"He has a hostage..." Sergeant Hurley called...

"Attention all units – hostage situation in progress at 659 West Avenue – Sergeant Hurley and Officer Nelson on the scene..."

"I'm Della Crews, News 12 Connecticut. We interrupt our regularly scheduled program to bring you the following: Police in Milford are responding to a report of shots being fired near West Avenue in Milford. News 12 has also been advised that there is a hostage situation in progress. We will continue to bring you updates. We now return to our regularly scheduled programming..."

"Give me my phone..." Darien said...

"What are you doing?"

"I'm calling Lacey..." Darien said as he dialed Lacey's number...

"Your phone's ringing..." Dexter said as he picked it up... "Oh look – your husband decided to join the party... "Hello Darien..."

"Where's my wife?"

"She's here..."

"Can I speak to her?"

"Did you call the police on me?"

"I didn't call the police – I didn't even know you were there!"

"Your wife let me in – just like she did when you came home early..."

"Darien – I'm sorry!" I cried...

"Bitch – shut the fuck up!" Dexter exclaimed as he slapped me...

"Aaaaggghhh!"

"Lacey!"

"I'm sorry... Lacey' busy now... she can't talk..." Dexter said as he hung up...

"What the fuck? You tryin' to come in the door? Oh hell no!" Dexter exclaimed as he started shooting at the door. I jumped up off the couch and ran into the bathroom as I heard the cops ramming the door with the battering ram... "Get your ass out here!" he exclaimed as he snatched me by my hair and dragged me out the bathroom...

"Let her go!" Sergeant Hurley yelled as the officers burst in...

"Drop your fuckin' weapons – now!" Dexter exclaimed as he put the gun to my head...

"Please don't kill me!"

"Okay – okay – I'm putting my gun down!" Sergeant Hurley yelled as he threw his gun down the stairs...

"Everybody get the fuck back!" Dexter snapped as he pushed the gun into my temple...

"Please don't kill me!"

"I told you shut the fuck up – now move!" he exclaimed as he dragged me towards the door... "Get the fuck back!"

"Okay – okay – get the fuck back!" Sergeant Hurley yelled. The officers backed down the stairs and backed out the door...

"Move!" Dexter exclaimed as he dragged me down the stairs and out the door...

"Jeremy – that's him – that's the man I saw this morning!" Alice yelled...

"Shut your fuckin' mouth Bitch!" Dexter yelled as he turned the gun away from me and pointed the gun at her...

"POW! POW! POW! POW!"

"LLLAAACCCEEEYYY!" Darien screamed as he jumped out the car and ran over to the building...

"DARIEN!" I yelled as I ran to him and collapsed in his arms...

"He's dead Sarge..." Officer Nelson said...

"Call it in..."

"Mutha Fuckaaaa!" I screamed as I ran over to Dexter and began kicking and stomping all over his body...

"Lacey – it's over – I gotchu..." Darien said as he ran up behind me and pulled me away from him...

"We need to get a statement..." Sergeant Hurley said...

"My wife's in no condition to give a statement..."

"Yes the hell I am!" I exclaimed...

"You need to go to the hospital – you're bleeding..."

"I don't need to go to the hospital – I need to be with my husband..."

"Lacey – I'll go to the hospital with you – I wanna make sure you're okay..."

"Darien... I'm sorry..."

"It's over..."

"I'm sorry..."

"Nelson – get them to the hospital..."

"We'll take our own car..." Darien said...

"Bazil – you comin'?"

"I'm coming..." he answered as they got in the car and drove off...

"Alice – who dat?"

"That's the man I saw jerkin' off in the car this mornin'!"

"You lyin'!"

"That's him..."

"I wonder what he was doin' upstairs?"

"Chile – her husband wasn't home – you know what that means..."

"No!"

"Yes girl!"

"You're the officer that shot him?" the ambulance tech asked...

"Yea..."

"I need your information for the report..."

"Here's my card..." Sergeant Hurley said as he gave him his card...

"Thanks – we'll call if we have any questions..." he said as he got in the ambulance and drove off...

"We have a gunshot victim coming in..." the tech said...

"Is that the one that got killed on West Avenue?"

"Yea – that's the one – his victim is coming in with her husband..." he said as we walked in...

"Any ID on the gun shot?"

"Yea – Dexter Alarie..."

"Alarie – he French?"

"Hell if I know..." the ambulance tech laughed...

"Hi – I'm Dr. Abreo – where you shot?" he asked...

"No – he just hit me upside my head with the gun..."

"Are you her husband?" he asked Bazil...

"No – I'm a friend..."

"I'm her husband..." Darien said as he stepped forward...

"I'm sorry – your friend needs to wait in the waiting room...

"That's fine..." Bazil said as he started to leave...

"Bazil – wait..." Darien said...

"We need to get your wife checked out..." Dr. Abreo said...

"I understand that – and I'd like my brother to come with us..."

"Your brother? Fine – come with me..." he said as we followed him to a bed...

"I'll be right back..." Dr. Abreo said as he went to check on another patient...

"Sure – go 'head – it's not like this is an emergency – mutha fucka just threatened to kill my wife – no big deal..." Darien said sarcastically...

"Mr. Beaufort?" Dr. Abreo asked as he turned around...

"Yea?"

"I understand you're upset – I also understand how serious this is – but your wife is alive – we have another patient that may not make it – so if you don't mind – or even if you do – I'll be right back..." he said as he went to check on the other patient..."

"Mutha fucka..." Darien mumbled...

"Darien – calm down..." Bazil said...

"You alright?" Darien asked me...

"My head hurts..."

"Hi – my name is Sharon – I'm going to be your nurse – I need to check your head and see if you need stiches..."

"Hi Sharon – I'm Lacey…"

"Hi Lacey – you must be her husband…" she said to Bazil…

"Why everybody think you're my wife's husband man?" Darien laughed…

"I have no idea!" Bazil laughed…

"Okay sir – who are you?"

"That's my brother Bazil – I'm Darien – I'm Lacey's husband…"

"Okay – got it – anybody take your information?"

"The police took it…" I said…

"I mean your insurance Maam…"

"Lacey…"

"Lacey – did anybody take your insurance?"

"Here…" Darien said as he took out the insurance card and handed it to her…

"I'm just gonna make a copy of this – I'll be right back…" she said as she left…

"Hello Mrs. Beaufort – has the nurse been to see you?" Dr. Abreo asked as he came back in…

"Yes – she's been here…"

"Mr. Beaufort – I'm sorry about earlier…"

"That's okay – how's the other patient doing?"

"He didn't make it…" Dr. Abreo answered as he went to see another patient…

"Okay – I'm back – let me take a look…" Sharon said as she came over to me and looked at my head... "This may sting a little..." she said as she applied whatever was on the cotton ball...

"Ouch!"

"Sorry – I gotta make sure it's clean..." she said as she continued cleaning my wound... "Okay – it doesn't look like you need stitches – but you do need to be careful – no salons for the next two weeks..."

"No salons?"

"No coloring, bleaching, chemical relaxers, etc..."

"Oh – okay – can I wash my hair?"

"Yes – you can wash your hair – at home..."

"Okay – can we go home now?"

"Yes – I'll get your papers..."

"Bazil! Where are you?" Beautiee asked...

"I'm at the hospital with Lacey and Darien..."

"Is she okay?"

"She's okay..."

"I miss you..."

"I miss you too... "

"I saw what happened..."

"You did?"

"News 12 has been running it – the kids got so excited because you were on tv..."

"I was?"

"Yea..."

"I didn't even realize News 12 was there..." Bazil laughed...

"It's on News 12?" Darien asked...

"Yea – Beautiee – le'me go – I'll talk to you later – okay?"

"Should I wait up?"

"Oh yea..."

"I love you..."

"I love you too..."

"I'm Della Crews, News 12 Connecticut. We interrupt our regularly scheduled programming to bring you this update. Earlier this evening, police responded to a report of shots being fired near West Avenue in Milford. At that time, there was a hostage situation in progress. It has now been confirmed that Dexter Alarie was holding a woman hostage and was killed at the scene. The hostage was taken to the hospital for minor injuries and released. There were no other fatalities. I'm Della Crews and you're watching News 12 Connecticut. We now return to our regularly scheduled programming..."

"Here's your release papers..." Sharon said as she came in...

"Thank God – where do I sign?"

"Sign here, and here – then you're free to go..."

"Not exactly..." Sergeant Hurley said as he came in...

"Hello Sergeant – I'm Darien..." Darien said as he extended his hand...

"Sorry to meet you under these circumstances..." he said as he shook Darien's hand...

"Hello Bazil..."

"Hello Jeremy..."

"Mrs. Beaufort – I need you to come down to the station and answer some questions..."

"Okay..." I sighed...

"I'ma go – call me if you need me..." Bazil said...

"Aiight – we'll talk..." Darien said as Bazil left and we followed Sergeant Hurley down to the station.

Chapter 13

"May I speak with you privately?" Sergeant Hurley asked...

"I'd like my husband to be with me..."

"Let me speak to you privately for a minute – then I'll come out and get your husband..."

"Why can't I go with my wife?"

"Darien – it's okay..."

'I'll be right here..." Darien said as we went inside the interrogation room...

"Hey..." Bazil whispered as he came into the bedroom...

"Hey..." Beautiee whispered back...

"I see you have company..."

"Yes..."

"How long have then been asleep?"

"About a half hour..."

"I'll put them to bed..."

"They missed you..."

"Aww..."

"They said they didn't want me to be lonely..." I said as Bazil took his phone out and took a picture...

"Really Bazil? My hair's a mess and my tittie's out!"

"All I see is my beautiful wife, with our beautiful children, breast-feeding our beautiful daughter..."

"Aww... I love you..."

"Look at Lydia - she's still on that tittie – even in her sleep..." Bazil laughed...

"They're so cute – the boys don't pay it any mind – but Joy's still fascinated with it..." Beautiee laughed...

"You only stopped breast-feeding her a little while ago..."

"I know – the only reason she stopped whining about it is because I tell her I only have enough milk for her sister..." Beautiee laughed... "And she wasn't the only one fascinated with it..."

"What do you mean?"

"After Jay was born, Starr was fascinated with breast feeding too – she would watch me breast-feed Jay and ask questions..."

"Really?"

"Yes – she asked me what it felt like, if it hurt, and she was curious about the taste – so I let her taste it..."

"You let Starr suck your tittie?"

"No! I took her hand, squeezed some milk out my nipple, and let her taste it that way..."

"I can't believe you breast-fed my daughter..."

"Does that bother you?"

"No... I think that's beautiful..."

"I love you..."

"I love you too..." Bazil said as he looked at her lovingly, touched her face, and started crying...

"Bazil – what's wrong?"

"Dexter hit Lacey with the butt of the gun..."

"Is she okay?"

"She's okay... it's just..."

"Bazil – what is it?"

"When I saw that... all I could think about was you... and..."

"Bazil... I'm fine..."

"When you were in prison – and I saw that video of you getting hit in the head with the chair... I wasn't able to protect you..."

"Bazil... don't cry..." she said as she started crying...

"I can't live without you..."

"Bazil... I'm not going anywhere..."

"I'm sorry... it's just that we've been through so much – and their situation is bringing up all these feelings..."

"I'm feeling something right now..."

"Oh yea?"

"Hurry up and put the kids to bed..."

"Okay..." Bazil said as he picked Jay up in his arms and took him to his room..."

"I wanted to talk to you privately because I got a hold of Dexter's phone..."

"Oohh..."

"He has a lot of videos..."

"I know..."

"Does your husband know you were having an affair with him?"

"Yes..." I sighed...

"I also wanted to ask you about this letter..." he said as he put the letter I wrote on the table...

"He made me write that..." I sighed...

"When I bring your husband in here – he's going to want to know what we talked about..."

"I know..."

"You still want me to get him?"

"Yes..."

"Okay – I'll be right back..."

"Now I'll put the last one to bed – I'll be right back..." Bazil said as he picked up Lydia and took her to her room, and came back. Bazil closed the door, locked it, got undressed, and climbed into bed... "Feed me..." he breathed as he took Beautiee's breast in his mouth...

"Bazil... leave some for your daughter... she'll be hungry in a few hours..."

'I'm hungry now..." he growled as he took her breast in his mouth" and licked and sucked...

"Lacey..." Darien sighed as he sat down beside me and pulled me to him...

"I'm okay..."

"Mr. Beaufort – I wanted to speak to your wife privately because... I'm sorry – there's no easy way to say this..."

"What's wrong Sergeant?"

"Sigh... we have Dexter's phone..."

"Ooohhh..."

"He has videos in his phone..."

"Videos of him... with my wife..."

"Yes..."

"Can these be deleted?"

"We can wipe the phone – but..."

"But what?"

"Well... most of the time – people with iPhones back up their data to the cloud..."

"What does that mean?"

"It means... even if we wipe the phone – the videos can still be retrieved by anyone that had access to his phone..."

"Oh my God!" I cried...

"I know no it sounds bad – but it may only be the people that manage the cloud – it doesn't necessarily mean other people..."

"Oh – so whoever's on shift at google gets free porn – featuring me – that's just fuckin' great!" I exclaimed...

"Lacey – don't cry – maybe he just saved them to his computer ..."

"You can wipe his computer – right Sergeant?" Darien asked...

"We can do that – but there's something else I need to show you..." Sergeant Hurley said as he put the letter on the table. Darien picked up the letter and started reading...

"Dear Darien, I love you with all my heart but I love Dexter too. I've tried to fight my feelings for him but I can't. It isn't fair to either one of you – so I've decided to follow my heart and go be with Dexter. Lacey..."

"So – you were leaving me? To be with him? Really?"

"He forced me to write that!"

"You could've just wrote I'm leaving – good bye – but all this about following your heart..." Darien said as he started tearing up...

"Darien – please – listen – I didn't mean it – he said I needed to convince him or he'd kill me – he had a gun pointed at me – I didn't mean it – I swear..."

"What if I never bought the security system? What if the police never showed up? What if he took you away from me and I never saw you again? I could've lost you!"

"I know – I'm sorry!" I cried...

"Sergeant Hurley – does this have to be in the report?" Darien asked...

"Yes..."

"Why?"

"Everytime an officer fires their weapon – they get interviewed – they have to make sure the shooting was justified – and they may question both of you..."

"Why?" I asked...

"They need to make sure what I told them is what actually happened..."

"What more do they need?!" I exclaimed...

"They need to see his phone..."

"Oh my God! Can you delete the videos?"

"As long as I'm under investigation – I can't delete anything – I'm sorry..."

"Do they have to watch them?"

"They don't have to watch them – but I can't delete them – those videos – along with the text messages between you – and the surveillance caught on camera by your husband – plus the testimony of your neighbor – you don't need to worry – I'll be fine – once Internal Affairs is satisfied – we can delete everything..."

"You said our neighbor – what's she got to do with this?" Darien asked...

"Earlier this morning – your neighbor Alice gave me a statement saying she saw Dexter jerkin' off in his car while he was watching a video on his phone..."

"Oh my God... I wanna die!"

"Lacey... Baby no... please don't say that..."

"She called me back because she went to the store to get cigarettes and saw his car parked around the corner – by that time – Dexter shot out two of your cameras – which leads me to my question – Mrs. Beaufort – why did you let him in?"

"I let him in because I'm a fuckin' idiot!"

"Lacey... no..." Darien said...

"Why did you let him in?"

"I told him to leave... but he refused... and then he sent another video to my phone..."

"Another one? So he sent you a video before?"

"Yes – when he blackmailed me – he threatened to send it to my husband unless I paid him $2,000..."

"According to the texts between you – that's when you met him at the Holiday Inn – is that correct?"

"Yes..."

"What about this morning?"

"He said if I didn't open the door... he'd send the video to my husband... and then after I let him in... he showed me all the videos he had... and he acted like he didn't remember which one it was... and then he told me he might have hit send my mistake..." I answered as I started crying again...

"Okay – that's all I need – are you up to talking to Internal Affairs?"

"Now?"

"I wouldn't ask – but the sooner you talk to them – the sooner I can delete those videos and make sure they don't go to the cloud..."

"She'll do it..." Darien said...

"Darien!"

"I'll be right there with you..."

"Mr. Beaufort – they may not let you..."

"They don't have a choice..."

"Okay – I'll let them know you're ready..."

"Bazil... Yes... Don't stop... Fuck..." Beautiee moaned as he continued licking and sucking her breast while fucking her harder... "Bazil... Don't stop... Fuck... I'm cumming... Haah... Haah... Haah... Haah... HHHAAAGGGHHH!" Bazil's body began to tense and Beautiee held him down on her breast as he started cumming...

"MMMPH! MMMPH! MMMPH! MMMPH! MMMPPPHHH!" Bazil slowed down but didn't stop as he continued licking and sucking on her breast for a few moments... and then he pulled her face to his, kissed her hard, pushed his tongue in her mouth, and tongued her down as she sucked the nectar of her breast milk off his tongue...

"Mr. & Mrs. Beaufort – I'm Lieutenant Starks – this is Lieutenant Simone – we're from Internal Affairs..." he said as he sat down. No eye contact. No smile. Cold...

"Hello Mrs. Beaufort – I'm Lieutenant Simone..." she said as she extended her hand to shake mine..."

"Mr. Beaufort – we'd prefer you wait outside..."

"No thank you..." Darien said...

"That wasn't a request..."

"I'm not speaking to you without my husband..." I said...

"Fine!" he said as he got up... "We'll get a court order..."

"Lieutenant – wait..." Lieutenant Simone said...

"Simone – you know how this works – he can't be in here!"

"Excuse us..." Lieutenant Simone said as she got up and they both went in the hallway...

"Don't ever question me in front of a suspect again!"

"First of all – she's not a suspect – she's a witness – second of all – shut up and put your dick back in your pants!"

"What the fuck did you just say to me?"

"You heard me!"

"I swear to God – this is why I don't like working with you Bitches!"

"Oh my God – you called me a Bitch –boo fucking whoo!"

"Look Simone..."

"No – you look – Bitch – I don't like you – nobody likes you – and you don't like me – we have a job to do – we came here to get a statement – she's willing to give it – let's do our job – get her statement – and then I can get the fuck away from you – okay?"

"Fine – you go talk to her then!"

"Fine by me!" she said and then she came back in the room...

"Are you okay?" I asked...

"I'm fine..."

"Does he always talk to you like that?" Darien asked...

"Look – I appreciate your concern – but..."

"I'm sorry – it's not my business..."

"That's okay – now let's get this statement..." she said as she set up the recorder... "Do you have any questions before I begin?"

"No..." I answered...

"I'm going to ask you some personal questions – they may be uncomfortable – I'm sorry – but I have to ask..."

"Okay..." I sighed as I squeezed Darien's hand...

"I'm Lieutenant Simone, Internal Affairs – I'm speaking with Mrs. Lacey Beaufort – this conversation is being recorded – Mrs. Beaufort – do you have any questions before we begin?"

"Can I go home?"

"As soon as we're done..." she laughed...

"I tried..."

"Mrs. Beaufort – according to Sergeant Hurley – you were being held hostage in your home at 659 West Avenue, Milford, Connecticut – is that correct?"

"Yes..."

"On the day in question – how did Mr. Alarie get into your apartment?"

"I let him in..." I sighed...

"Mrs. Beaufort – I have to ask – why did you let him in?"

"He sent a video to my phone..."

"What was in the video?"

"It was a video of us... having sex..."

"Did you let him in to have sex?"

"No!"

"Isn't it true you were having an affair with him?"

"Yes..."

"Okay – he sent the video to your phone – I still don't understand why you let him in..."

"He said if I didn't let him in... he'd send the video to my husband..."

"So – I want to make sure I understand you correctly – you thought if you let him in – he wouldn't send the video?"

"I know – I can't believe I was so fuckin' stupid!"

"Mrs. Beaufort – I'm not judging you – I just had to ask..."

"Okay..."

"What happened after you let him in?"

"He shot the camera we had in the kitchen... he tried to kiss me... I pushed him off me... he said he'd delete the video... and then he showed me his phone..."

"Did you ever consent to being recorded?'

"No!"

"What about this?" she asked as she put the letter on the table...

"Dear Darien, I love you with all my heart but I love Dexter too. I've tried to fight my feelings for him but I can't. It isn't fair to either one of you – so I've decided to follow my heart and go be with Dexter. Lacey..."

"He put a gun in my waist... he forced me to write that..."

"Are you sure you wrote this because he forced you to write it?"

"Yes!"

"Did he tell you what to write?'

"No..."

"So – Mrs. Beaufort – if he told you to write a letter – why not just say I'm leaving to be with Dexter?"

"He said I needed to convince him... or he was gonna kill me..."

"What happened after you wrote the letter?"

142

"He pushed me down on the couch... he lay on top of me... he said he still wasn't convinced... he started kissing me... the cops began banging on the door... I jumped up... I tried to run... he grabbed me by my hair... he pushed the gun in my head..." I answered as I started to cry...

"Lacey..." Darien whispered as he wiped my tears...

"Mrs. Beaufort – I need you to finish telling me what happened..."

"He told Sergeant Hurley to drop the gun... Sergeant Hurley threw his gun downstairs... he told the cops to get the fuck back... he dragged me downstairs by my hair..."

"Mrs. Beaufort – did Sergeant Hurley get his gun?"

"No..."

"Mrs. Beaufort – to the best of your recollection – when did Sergeant Hurley get his gun?"

"Dexter dragged me outside... he had the gun to my head... I heard Alice say that's the man she saw earlier... he took the gun away from my head and pointed it at Alice... he said Bitch shut your fuckin' mouth... and that's when he was shot..."

"Did you see Sergeant Hurley shoot him?"

"No..."

"How did you know he was shot?"

"The other officer came up on the landing and said he was dead..."

"Thank you Mrs. Beaufort – I don't have any more questions..." she said as she stopped recording...

"Can I go home now?"

"Yes – you can go home – if we need anything else – we'll call you..." she said as she opened the briefcase, put the recorder in it, put the microphone it it, closed it, got up, and left...

"Darien... I'm so sorry..." Darien pulled me into a kiss and kissed me so hard he startled me...

"Okay... I'll stop talking..." I breathed as he kissed me again...

"BBBAAAZZZIIILLL!! I'M CUMMING!! AAAGGGHHH!!"

"UUUGGGHHH!! UUUGGGHHH!! UUUGGGHHH!!!"

"Oh my God..." Beautiee breathed..."

"I know..." Bazil breathed...

"I love it...." she breathed...

"What?"

"Whatever's gotten into you..." she breathed as she pulled him into a kiss.

Chapter 14

When we got out the car I ran to Alice as soon as I saw her... "Alice! Alice!"

"Lacey!" she exclaimed as she ran towards me...

"Thank you!" I exclaimed as I grabbed her and hugged her...

"You ain't mad?"

"Why would I be mad?"

"Well – you always say I need to mind my business..."

"Thank God you're nosy!" I laughed...

"Alright – you welcome – but you remember that the next time you get mad at me for minding y'alls business..."

"Alice – you can mind our business anytime..." Darien said as he walked up to her, took her face in his hands... and kissed her in the mouth...

"Oh hell no – I don't get down like that – nice lips though..."

"Thank you..." Darien laughed...

"Y'all alright?"

"Yea..."

"Y'all talk to Jeremy?"

"Who's Jeremy?" I asked...

"Sergeant Hurley..."

"You're on a first name basis with him?" Darien asked...

"Sho am – he gave me his card – said I could call him anytime..."

"Good for you..." Darien said...

"I sho hope so!" Alice laughed...

"Well – we gotta get upstairs – we'll see you later..." Darien said as he took my hand and we went upstairs. When we got to the door Darien looked up at the top of the door where the camera was and shook his head before he pulled the crime tape away from the door and pushed it open. When we got inside, Darien looked around the living room and saw that the camera was still in tact... "Hmmm – he didn't see this one..."

"I kept his attention so he wouldn't..."

"Was he in our bedroom?"

"No..."

"I'm going in the kitchen..." he said as he went into the kitchen... "Lacey?"

"Yes Darien?" I answered as I came in the kitchen...

"Are you hungry?"

"Kinda..."

"I'll make us something to eat..." he said as he went to the sink, washed his hands, dried them, and went into the refrigerator... "We still have some Italian bread – I'll make us an Italian club..."

"Okay..." Darien took the bread, mayonnaise, balsamic, ham, pepperoni, capicola, soppressata, genoa salami, prosciutto, and provolone out the refrigerator, took two plates out the cabinet, and I watched him as he made our sandwiches. After he was done, he put everything back in the refrigerator and brought the plates to the table...

"That looks really good..."

"You're welcome..." he said as he went into the refrigerator... "Carona or moscato?"

"Carona..."

"Okay..." he said as he took two bottles out the refrigerator, brought them to the table, and popped the caps off of them. Darien went over to the cabinet, took down two glasses, brought them to the table, and poured the beer in our glasses...

"Lacey?" he asked as we started eating..."

"Yes Darien?"

"The doctor said everything's fine..."

"Oh thank God!" I exclaimed as I went to hug him and he stopped me...

"Sit down and finish eating Lacey..."

"Okay..."

"Dr. Har said as men, we get so caught up in satisfying our ladies that we forget we need to be satisfied too..."

"I don't satisfy you?"

"Let me finish..."

"Okay..."

"I've been under a lot of pressure at work lately..."

"Why didn't you tell me?"

"I didn't want to tell you I was under pressure at work – I wanted to come home, eat, have a few drinks, and enjoy being with my wife..."

"I wish you had told me..."

"I wish I had told you too – I never thought it would push you to another man – and then on top of that – you fell in love with him..."

"I'm sorry..."

"I know you are – but it doesn't change what happen..."

"I know..."

"The camera's been shot by the door – the camera's been shot by the kitchen – and he was in here again – and he got in here because you let him in here – again!" he gritted as he banged his fist on the table...

"Darien... please... I'm sorry..."

'I'm sorry too – I'm sorry I didn't bounce his ass down the fuckin' stairs when I saw him in our bedroom..."

"Why didn't you do that then?"

"Because you wanted him!"

"I thought you said you forgive me?"

"I do – but you hurt me – and I'm angry..."

"I'm..."

"Don't fuckin' say it!"

"Okay..." I whispered as I started crying...

"I think we should put having a baby on hold..."

"Darien... No..."

"Just for now..."

"We were doing so good – I thought..."

"I thought so too – until I saw that letter..."

"HE MADE ME WRITE THAT!" I screamed...

"Who are you trying to convince – me – or yourself?"

"DARIEN!"

"You said it wasn't fair to him – or me – you said you had to follow your heart... where is your heart Lacey?"

"My heart is here! With you!"

"Is it?"

"What's that supposed to mean?"

"How can your heart be here with me when you loved both of us?"

"It wasn't like that!"

"What was it like Lacey?"

"I can't explain it..."

"You enjoyed having sex with him – didn't you?"

"Yes..." I whispered...

"We've been having sex often..."

"I know..."

"I've enjoyed it..."

"I've enjoyed it too..."

"We're you sexing me the way you've been sexing me because you love me – or was it because you felt guilty?"

"Both..." I sighed as I slumped down in the chair...

"That's what I thought..." he said as he got up to leave...

"Where are you going?"

"I'm going out – I'll be back later..." he said as he left...

"Hello..." I answered...

"Mrs. Beaufort – this is Sergeant Hurley..."

"Hello..."

"I'm calling to let you know Internal Affairs cleared me..."

"That's great..."

"Since they cleared me – I can wipe Dexter's phone and clean out his computer..."

"That's good..."

"I checked his account – he didn't back up anything to google so you don't have to worry about your videos in the cloud..."

"They weren't my videos..."

"I'm sorry – I didn't mean it that way – I just meant that the videos will be deleted..."

"Thank you..."

"You're welcome..." he said and then he hung up...

"Hey..." Bazil answered... "How's Lacey?"

"I don't know..."

"What's wrong?"

"I left..."

"Where are you?"

"Thirty Three..."

"I'm on my way – Beautiee – I gotta go..." he said as he grabbed his keys..."

"I hurt him so bad..." I slurred as I sipped the bottle of moscato... "Stupid Bitch – that's what I get for being so fuckin' stupid!" I slurred as I turned the bottle up... "Darien was so good to me – but that wasn't good enough for me – I had to go fuck somebody else!" I said as I turned the bottle up again... "Come to my house I said – it'll be exciting I said – my husband won't be home for a while I said – stupid, stupid, stupid!" I slurred as I turned the bottle up again... "Darien comes home – catches us – what do I do – I fuck them both – stupid! Stupid! Stupid!" I slurred as I turned the bottle up again... "No wonder he doesn't want a baby with me – I don't even want a baby with me!" I slurred as I turned the bottle up and it was empty... "Oh great – fuckin' great – too stupid to make sure I have another bottle of wine..."

"Darien..." Bazil said as he went up to the bar...

"It's over man..." Darien said as he started crying...

"What happened?"

"How much time you have?"

"Come sit with me..." Bazil said as he helped Darien down off the stool...

"Woa..." Darien laughed...

"I see you started without me..."

"Yea... sorry 'bout that..."

"Okay..." Bazil said as they sat down... "What happened?"

"This morning – our neighbor Alice caught this mutha fucka sitting in front of the house jerkin' his dick off to a video on his phone!"

"Oh shit!"

"He was waiting for me to leave!"

"Damn!"

"So Sergeant Hurley saw her goin' off and she told him what she saw..."

"He planned it?"

"He moved the car around the corner and came back after I left – by the time I saw him on surveillance – Alice had already called Sergeant Hurley to report she saw the car – and someone else called to say they heard gunshots..."

"You got there in time..."

"She let him in..."

"She let him in? Why?"

"He sent another video to her phone – he told her if she didn't let him in – he'd send it to me..."

"Fuck it – you already knew about the affair – she should've just told him fuck you!"

"You feel me?"

"I feel you – but I also know she didn't want to let him in..."

"He had a gun on her..."

"I know..."

"He forced her to write a letter telling me she was leaving me for him..."

"Darien – you know she didn't want to write that letter..."

"You didn't see what she wrote..."

"What'd she write?"

"She said she loved us both but she had to follow her heart because it wasn't fair to either one of us so she was leaving me for him..."

"What the fuck?"

"She said he told her she had to convince him or he'd kill her..."

"You don't believe her?"

"No..."

"You really think she wanted to be with Dexter?"

"How can she tell me she loves me and wants to be with me but then write a letter saying she has to follow her heart and be with him?"

"Darien – she was talking to you..."

"What?"

"She said she loved you both but she had to follow her heart..."

"Yea – she chose him!"

"She didn't choose him – she chose you..."

"Remember when I said she was sexin' me because she felt guilty?"

"Yea..."

"She admitted it!"

"Why would she feel guilty if she didn't love you?"

"She loved him too..."

"If she loved him – she'd be with him..."

"She told me she loved him!"

"She doesn't love him – she fucked him and caught feelings – there's a difference..."

"I love her so much..."

"I know you love her – but do you want her?"

"Yes... I want her..."

"C'mon..." Bazil laughed as he helped Darien up and they went to the parking lot...

"Fuck this!" I said as I got up and stumbled to the bedroom... "Oh God... my head's spinning... I need to lie down..." I said as I fell down on the bed, my arm hit the night stand, I knocked the bottle of Tylenol over, the cap fell off, and pills spilled all over the floor as I fell into a drunken stupor...

"I need to fix my door..."

"Not today – you're drunk..." Bazil laughed...

"I'm alright!" Darien laughed...

"Give me your keys..." Bazil laughed...

"How am going to get home?"

"I'll drop you off..." Bazil answered as he opened the door...

"What about my car?"

"I'll make sure you get your car..." Bazil said as they drove off.

Chapter 15

"C'mon..." Bazil laughed as he helped Darien out the car...

"I love you man..." Darien slurred...

"I love you too – but I need you to help me get you upstairs..." Bazil laughed as they got up the steps to the landing...

"I'm good..." Darien laughed as he opened the door...

"Are you sure?"

"I'm good!" Darien laughed as he tripped on the first step...

"See – I knew it – come on..." Bazil said as he put Darien's arm around him and help him upstairs. When they got to the door, Darien sighed...

"See that camera?"

"You can replace the camera – but you can't replace Lacey..."

"You're right..." he said as they came in the door...

"What's that smell?" Bazil asked...

"Lacey? Lacey – where are you? Oh shit – the smell's getting stronger... Oh my God –

LACEY!" Darien yelled as he rushed into the room with Bazil coming in behind him...

"Oh God... I threw up... I'm sorry..." I slurred...

"Lacey – how many pills did you take?" he asked as he grabbed me up in his arms...

"Darien – let's get her in the shower..." Bazil said as he came over to help Darien pick me up...

"Nooo... I don't wanna take a shower with Bazil..."

"How many pills did you take Lacey?" Darien asked...

"Put her in the water..." Bazil said as they both put me under the shower head...

"Nooo... I don't wanna take a shower with Bazil..."

"I'll go clean up..." Bazil said as he left the bathroom and went back to the bedroom...

"Lacey – I need to get you outta these clothes..."

'I don't wanna take a shower with Bazil..."

"Bazil's not here – it's just me..." he said as he held me under the water...

"I'm sorry Darien..." I cried...

"How many pills did you take?"

"I didn't take any pills... I'm drunk..."

"So am I..." he laughed...

"Oh God... Darien... UUUUGGGHHHH!" I heaved as I threw up again...

"How much did you have to drink?"

157

"The whole bottle..."

"Darien?"

"Yea Bazil?"

"Can I come in?"

"Yea..."

"Is she alright?" Bazil asked as he stuck his head in the bathroom...

"She's drunk..." Darien laughed...

"I don't wanna take a shower with you Bazil... oh God... my head..."

'I'ma take this out to the garbage – I'll call you later..." Bazil said as he left...

"Hello Mr. Osgood..."

"Mike – I need your help – I'm coming to pick you up..."

"You don't want me to drive?"

"No – I'm on my way..." he said and then he hung up and called Beautiee...

"Hey..." she sighed...

"Hey..."

"Is he alright?"

"He's drunk..." Bazil laughed...

"Oh God – you didn't let him drive did you?"

"No – I'm on my way to pick up Mike – I'm gonna have him drive Darien's car back, then Ill drop him off, and then I'll be home..."

"Okay... I love you..."

"I love you too – and Beautiee?"

"Yes Bazil?"

"Let the kids know they don't have to worry about you being lonely tonight..."

"Okay..."

"Lacey – I need to get you out of these clothes..." Darien said as he started to undress me...

"Darien... Nooo..."

"Lacey – I'm not going to hurt you..."

"You're not going to make me take a shower with Bazil?"

"Bazil's not here Lacey..." he said as he removed my bra and then my panties...

"Okay..." I sighed as I leaned into him...

"Lacey – I need you to stay awake..."

"I'm tired..." I sighed as he started washing my hair... "Ooohhh... that feels nice..." Darien took his time washing and conditioning my hair and then he lathered up the loofa and began washing my body...

"Hey Mr. Osgood..." Mike said as Bazil pulled up...

"Hey Mike..." Bazil said as Mike opened the door and got in...

"Where are we going?" Mike asked...

"Thirty Three..."

"I like that bar..."

"Me too..." When they got to the parking lot Bazil said, "I need you to take these keys – they go to that car over there – I need you to drive the car over to 659 West Avenue and park it...

"Okay Boss..."

"Darien... that feels good..." I said as he got out the shower with me, wrapped me in a towel, and dried my hair. Darien picked me up in his arms, carried me to the bed, laid me down, and turned to go back to the bathroom... "Darien – where are you going?"

"I need to get outta these clothes and take a shower – I'll be right back..."

"Thanks Mike..." Bazil said...

"You're welcome..."

"I'm going to go upstairs and give him his keys – I'll be right back..." Bazil said as he got out the car and headed upstairs... "Darien! It's me!"

"Bazil?"

"Yea!"

"Hang on a minute..." Darien said as he jumped out the shower, grabbed a robe, and went to open the door... "Hey!"

"Here's your keys..."

"You got the car? Already? Thanks man!" Darien said as he pulled Bazil into a hug...

"How's Lacey?"

"She's sleeping..."

"She's alright?"

"Yea... she's alright..."

"She didn't take any pills?"

"Naaa..."

"Good – I'ma go – call me if you need me..." Bazil said as he left...

"Darien..."

"Sssshhh..." he breathed in my ear as he held me...

"I love you..."

"I love you too..."

"I'm sorry..."

"I know... go back to sleep..." he said as he spooned me and we both fell asleep...

"Hey..." Bazil said as he came into the bedroom and started taking off his clothes...

"Hey..." Beautiee sighed...

"I need to talk to you..." he said as he walked past Beautiee, put on a robe, and sat down on the bed...

"What's wrong?"

"You want something to drink?"

"No..."

"You hungry?"

"Bazil – what happened?"

"Sigh... I went to the bar – he was drunk..."

"Yes – I know..."

"He was really messed up behind what happened..."

"I bet..."

"She let him in the house..."

"Why?"

"Because Dexter sent another video to her phone..."

"Ooohhh..."

"He said if she didn't let him in – he'd send it to Darien..."

"So she let him in..." Beautiee sighed...

"Yea..."

"I might've done the same thing..."

"Really?"

"Yea – how would you feel if you got a video of me fuckin' somebody else?"

"A video of you with Dontress would've been nice..."

"Bazil!"

"Well? What'd you expect me to say?"

"Never mind..." I laughed...

"Something else happened that fucked him up..."

"What?"

"After she let him in – he showed her he had a lot of videos in his phone..."

"He was recording her the whole time?"

"He also made her write a letter to Darien saying she was leaving him – so she wrote that she loved them both but she had to follow her heart..."

"She wasn't talking about Dexter when she said that – she was talking about Darien..."

"That's what I told him – but he doesn't believe her – at least he didn't believe her when I got there..."

"He's fucked up because he loves her..."

"I need you to talk to her..."

"Why? What happened?"

"Darien was drunk so I helped him upstairs..."

"Okay..."

"When we got inside – there was a really bad smell..."

"Oh God..."

"We went to the bedroom... Lacey was on her stomach – she threw up – and pills were all over the floor..."

"Oh my God! She tried to commit suicide?"

"That's what we thought at first..."

"So she didn't try to kill herself?"

"She was drunk... I helped Darien pick her up... and..."

"Bazil..." Beautiee said as she put her hand on his shoulder... "What happened?"

"She thought we were trying to take a shower with her..." he sighed...

"What?"

"She was drunk – she had vomit all over her – I was just trying to help Darien get her in the shower..."

"Bazil – I know..."

"She kept saying noooo... I don't wanna take a shower with Bazil..."

"Come here..." Beautiee said as she lay back against the headboard, pulled Bazil down, and held him...

"I'd never hurt her..."

"I know..."

"I'm gonna talk to Darien..."

"I wouldn't..."

"You don't think I should say anything?"

"No..."

"What if Darien says something?"

"He's not..."

"I love you..."

"I love you too – come to bed..." she said as she slid down under the covers. Bazil stood up, took off his robe, pulled back the covers, got in bed, and pulled Beautiee into a kiss.

Chapter 16

"Darien... Haah... Haah... Haah..."

"Fuck... Lacey... Shit..."

"I'm cumming... I'm cumming... I'm cumming..."

"Uggh! Uggh! Uggh! Uggh! Uggh!"

"AAAAGGGGHHHH!!!"

"UUUUGGGGHHHH!!!"

"That was so fucking good..." I panted...

"Yes..." Darien breathed as he kissed me...

"You're still hard..."

"I am..."

"You want more?"

"Yeesss..." he breathed as he pulled his dick out my pussy and eased it into my ass...

"Ooohhh..."

"Am I hurting you?"

"Nooo..." I moaned...

"Damn this feels good..."

"Fuck my ass Darien..." I moaned. Darien kissed me hard, pushed his tongue in my mouth, picked up my legs, pushed his dick in further, and fucked my ass harder...

"MMMPH! MMMPH! MMMPH! MMMPH! MMMPH!"

"MMMMM! MMMMM! MMMMM! MMMMM! MMMMM!"

"LACEY... LACEY... LACEY... LACEY... LLLAAACCCEEEYYY!!!" Darien slowed down but didn't stop as he started kissing me again. I felt so good, I silently thanked God for bringing us back together... "Are you okay?" he breathed...

"Yes..." I answered with tears in my eyes...

"Lacey... what's wrong?"

"Nothing..." I breathed as I pulled him into a kiss..."

"C'mon – let's get up – I'll make breakfast – and we can talk..."

"Okay..." I sighed. I was a little worried but I figured the way our morning started we'd be fine – I hoped... "We fucked on top of the mattress..."

"Yes... we did..."

"We messed it up..." I laughed...

"Yes... we did..."

"Look at that..." I said as I pointed to the wet spot. Darien came over to me, pulled me into a kiss, and whispered in my ear...

"We're going to make another one later..."

"Okay..." I giggled...

"C'mon..." he said as he opened the robe for me and helped me put it on...

"Okay..." I sighed as we walked through the living room and into the kitchen together...

"Have a seat..." he said as he pulled out the chair for me. I sat down and then he sat down...

"Yes Darien?"

"I'm sorry..."

"Darien... No..."

"Lacey – let me finish..."

"Okay..."

"I'm sorry for what happened yesterday after we got home – instead of yelling at you – I should've been comforting you..."

"Oh Darien... I love you so much..."

"I know you love me Lacey – I love you too – I just got fucked up – but I won't do that again – I promise..."

"Darien..." I whispered as I started to cry...

"Now – I need to talk to you about what you said at the precinct yesterday..."

"Okay..."

"You said you wanted to die..."

"I know..." I sighed...

"When we came in here – and we found you – I saw the pills on the floor... and..."

"Oh Darien – I didn't take any pills – I wasn't trying to kill myself – I swear..."

"Promise me you'll never say that to me again..."

"I promise – I'll never say that to you again..."

"I can't lose you Lacey..."

"You won't – I swear..."

"I need to tell you something..."

"Okay..."

"When we found you – you had thrown up – it was all over the bed – Bazil helped me get you in the shower..."

"Bazil was here?"

"Yes –he was here..."

"Oh my God – I don't remember..."

"Lacey – when Bazil was helping me put you in the shower – you kept saying nooo... I don't wanna take a shower with Bazil..."

"Oh My God!"

"Even after Bazil left – I started to undress you – you asked me if I was going to make you take a shower with Bazil..."

"Oh my God!"

"You didn't start to relax until I told you Bazil wasn't here..."

"Oh my God – I'm so embarrassed – I'll apologize to him..."

"You don't remember that?"

"No!"

"Bazil helped me put you in the shower – you were so drunk you could barely talk – except to say you were drunk..."

"Oh my God – I don't remember any of that!"

"Do you remember drinking?"

"Yea..."

"That was my fault..."

"I thought I lost you..."

"I thought I lost you too..."

"I need to tell you something..."

"Hold that thought – I'ma make us some coffee..." he said as he got up from the table. I watched Darien get the cups, put the kettle on, and make the coffee...

"Here..." he said as he put the cups on the table...

"Thank you..."

"What did you want to tell me?"

"Sergeant Hurley called me..."

"What'd he say?"

"He said Internal Affairs cleared him..."

"That's good..."

"He said now that he's cleared - he can wipe Dexter's phone and computer..."

"Good..."

"And guess what?"

"What?"

"Sergeant Hurley checked his account on google – Dexter didn't back anything up to the cloud..."

"Thank God!"

"Darien?"

"Yes Lacey?"

"I still wanna have a baby..."

"Me too..."

"You do?"

"Lacey – I said we should put it on hold – I didn't say it would be forever..." I sat there quiet, sipping my coffee. And then I bust out laughing...

"What's so funny?"

"You kissed Alice yesterday..." I laughed...

"Sorry about that..."

"I'm not..."

"You're not mad?"

"No Darien..."

"I didn't plan it – I was just so happy..."

"I know..."

"We'll be the topic of gossip for the summer..." he laughed...

"I know!" I laughed...

"I'ma make us some breakfast..."

"Okay..."

"Girl – what happened yesterday?" Shirley asked...

"I came downstairs to put my grandchil'ren on the bus – I came back and that man was jerkin' his dick and watching a video!"

"Oh my God – right outside?"

"Yes girl!"

"I would'a beat his ass!"

"Girl hush – he was in the car with the door locked..."

"You should'a broke the glass!"

"I banged on it – I called him a nasty mutha fucka!"

"I bet you did!"

"Jeremy came by and took a report..."

"Who's Jeremy?"

"Sergeant Hurley..."

"You got you a Sergeant?"

"I ain't say all that..." Alice laughed...

"You ain't have to – I know you!" Shirley laughed...

"He was holdin' Lacey hostage in her house..."

"No! You think they was fuckin'?"

"I know they were..."

"How you know?"

"How you think he got in they house – you know you gotta have a key – these doors can't be kicked in..."

"Oh my God! If I had a man like Darien – I'd rid his dick every chance I got!" she laughed...

"Girl hush!"

"You'd do the same thing to that Sergeant if you had the chance..." she laughed...

"Sho would!" Alice agreed... "I wonder if his lips as nice as Darien's?"

"Whatchu know about Darien's lips?"

"As soon as they got back here yesterday – Lacey runs to me, gives me a hug, thanks me for being nosey – and Darien kissed me!"

"What?"

"Yes girl!"

"Wait – Lacey thanked you – for being nosey? And Darien kissed you?"

"Ain't that what I said?"

"Damn – they a couple of freaks!" she said as they both laughed...

"That was delicious –thank you..." I said as I rubbed my stomach...

"You're welcome..." Darien said as he smiled mischievously and got up from the table...

"Come with me..." he said as he took my hand..."

"Okay..." I got up and Darien walked me into the bedroom, pushed my robe off my shoulders, and kissed me... "Mmmm...." I moaned...

"Today... I want to fix the door..." he said as he kissed my neck...

"Okay..."

"And I want to replace the cameras..."

"Okay..."

"And... since you want a camera in the bedroom..."

"Yeesss..."

"I want to buy a video camera..."

"Okay..."

"I want to set it up..."

"Okay..."

"And I want to punish you... on camera..." he breathed as he picked me up, wrapped my legs around him, and carried me into the shower.

Chapter 17

"What are you doing?" Bazil asked as he walked into the library...

"I'm working on some edits..."

"What's this book about?" Bazil asked as he sat down and looked over Beautiee's shoulder...

"It's about Lacey and Dexter..."

"Really?"

"Well – not specifically – but this author wrote a similar story – and they didn't have a happy ending..."

"Ooohhh... damn..."

"It's fun and exciting in the beginning – but it's not worth the consequences..."

"You're right...."

"People catch feelings – shit goes left – and then shit gets crazy – especially when the sex is good..."

"I guess what you're saying is you'd never go for that..." Bazil laughed...

"Did you forget what happened to MaryJane LaRue?" Beautiee snapped...

"Come here..." Bazil breathed as he pulled her into a kiss and held her... "I didn't mean to upset you...

"I'm sorry..."

"You don't need to apologize – I shouldn't've brought it up...

"You belong to me..."

"Yes... I belong to you..." Bazil breathed as he kissed her...

"We need to update the virus protection on our computer before it expires..."

"We can go to Best Buy..."

"Can we go to Longhorn Steakhouse?"

"We can do that..." Bazil breathed as he pulled Beautiee up out the chair, led her to the sofa, sat her down, and pushed her back...

"Bazil..."

"Yeessss..."

"We need to get ready..."

"I am ready..." he breathed as he lay on top of her and spread her legs...

"You ready?" Darien asked as he came up behind me and kissed me on my neck...

"Darien... stop..."

"Why?" he breathed as he turned me around, bent me back on the dresser, and kissed me hard...

"Darien... stop..."

"Why?" he breathed as he began running his hands up and down my body...

"Darien... stop..."

"What if I don't want to?"

"We won't get outta here..."

"So..." he breathed as he started unbuttoning my blouse...

"Darien... I... I..."

"Yes Lacey..." he breathed as he kissed my breasts through my bra...

"I want..."

"Yes..." he breathed as he took my breast out and started sucking it...

"Camera..." I breathed...

"Okay..." he breathed as he kissed me again... "We'll wait..."

"Okay..." I breathed. Darien was enjoying the fact that he had me flustered and he bust out laughing...

"C'mon..." I sighed as I went towards the door and waited...

"I'm sorry – I thought it was funny..."

"I know..."

"You still love me?"

"If I said no – would you believe me?"

"Hell no!" he laughed as we went out, locked the door, and went downstairs...

"Hey Lacey – you alright?" Shirley asked...

"I'm okay – thanks..."

"Good thing Alice nosey huh?"

"Alice isn't really nosey – she's just the Captain..."

"Captain? Of what?"

"Neighborhood Watch..." I answered as we got in the car...

"You know she's gonna tell Alice what you said..." Darien laughed...

"Yes..." I laughed...

"I can't wait to get the camera..." he said as we rode...

"Me either..."

"Welcome to Best Buy – oh hello Mr. & Mrs. Osgood..." the customer service technician beamed... "What can we do for you?"

"We need to update our virus protection on our computer..." Beautiee answered...

"Did you buy it here last year?"

"Yes..."

"Let me see if we can update you from here..." he said as we followed him to the customer service area...

"You can do that from the computer?"

"Yes – if you save us your credit card and we stored it – we can renew it automatically..."

"Oh that's nice..." Bazil said...

"Welcome to Best Buy – how can I help you?" the customer service technician asked...

"I need to replace two of our security cameras..." Darien answered...

"I can help you with that – what system are you using?"

"Simply Safe..."

"Where the cameras damaged when you purchased your system?"

"No..."

"Do you have the damaged cameras with you?"

"No..."

"Okay – let's go get your cameras – with there be anything else?"

"Yes – we'd like a hand-held video camera..."

"You came in at the right time – we have the Sony Handycam Flash Memory camcorder on sale – it's $679.99 – regular price is $849.99..."

"That sounds good..." Darien said as he held the camera and looked at it...

"You can purchase it out right or we have 18-month financing for $37.78 a month..."

"Has it been rated?"

"Yes – so far it has 573 reviews – the average rating is between 4 and 5..."

"Does it come with a tripod?" I asked...

"You can purchase that separately for $99.99..."

"Is there a warranty?"

"Yes – but you can purchase additional protection if you want – 1 year, 2 years, or 3 years..."

"Let's get it..." I said...

"Okay! I'll get your items – meet me over at customer service..." he said he went to get our cameras and we went over to customer service...

"Mr. & Mrs. Osgood – you're all set..." the customer service technician said as he came out...

"Great – thank you..." Bazil said...

"You're welcome – in the future – you can just click on the link in your email and it will automatically renew so you don't have to come to the store..."

"Thanks again..." Bazil said...

"Hey guys!" Darien said as we saw Bazil and Beautiee...

"Lacey!" Beautiee exclaimed as she pulled me into a hug...

"Hi Beautiee..."

"Hi Darien..." Beautiee said...

"Good to see you – did you get your cameras?" Bazil asked...

"Yes..."

"Bazil – I'm sorry..." I sighed... "Darien told me what happened – I was so drunk I didn't even remember you were there – I'm so embarrassed..."

"Don't be – it's okay..." Bazil said...

"We've all been there..." I laughed...

"What bring you here?" Darien asked...

"We needed to update our virus protection – we can't afford for anything to happen to our computers..." Beautiee said...

"Especially because Beautiee's working from home..." Bazil said...

"You're all set – will this be cash or charge?" the customer service technician asked...

"Charge..." Darien answered as he handed the technician his card...

"Thank you Mr. Beaufort – I'll be right back..." he said as he went to ring us up...

"We're going to Longhorn Steakhouse – come with us..." Beautiee said...

"Okay!" I exclaimed...

"Here you go Mr. Beaufort – have a nice day..."

"Thanks – you too..." Darien said as we all left Best Buy, headed to the parking lot, and went over to Longhorn Steakhouse...

"Hello?" Alice answered...

"Hello Alice – this is Sergeant Hurley..."

"Hi Jeremy..." Alice beamed as Shirley listened...

"Listen – I was calling to thank you for all your help..."

"You're welcome...

"What time is it now?"

"It's a little after 12..."

"What time do you pick up your grandchildren?"

"I go to the corner at 3..."

"I'm about to break for lunch – would you like to have lunch with me?"

"Sho would!"

"Okay – I'll be there in a few minutes..."

"I'm not dressed – I don't have nothin' fancy..."

"You don't need to dress fancy – just put on whatever..."

"Okay Jeremy – I'll see you in a few minutes..."

"Girl! You got you a Sergeant!"

"Listen – I can't talk now – I need to go get dressed..." Alice said as she went upstairs. Sergeant Hurley was downstairs waiting when Alice came downstairs and the neighbors were all chattering...

"Ohhh – Alice gettin' arrested?"

"Oh shit – that's the one that arrested that guy the other day!"

"Maybe Alice is a witness!"

"I hope she ain't hit one a dem parents – you know she don't play when it comes to her grandkids..."

"I know – right?"

"Y'all hush – Alice is going on a date!" Shirley said...

"Mind yo' business!" Alice yelled as she got in the car...

"Hello Alice..."

"Hello Jeremy..."

"Thank you for going to lunch with me..."

"Thank you for asking..."

"Where would you like to go?"

"I'on know..."

"What would you like to eat?"

"I like shrimp..."

"I have an idea..." Sergeant Hurley said as he put the car in drive and took off...

"Welcome to Longhorn Steakhouse – how many people are in your party?" the hostess asked...

"Four..." Bazil answered...

"Come with me..." she said as she picked up four menus and then we followed her...

"Welcome to Longhorn Steakhouse – table for two?"

"Yes Maam..." Sergeant Hurley answered...

"Right this way..." the hostess said as they followed her and they were seated right across from us...

"Sergeant Hurley!" I exclaimed...

"Hello Mrs. Beaufort, Mr. Beaufort – hello Bazil, Beautiee..."

"Beautiee – that's Alice – she helped save my life..." I said as I teared up...

"Lacey you goin' make my cry..." Alice said...

"We have room at our table – please – join us..." Darien said...

"Okay..." Sergeant Hurley sighed as they got up and joined us...

"Alice – come sit here!" I said as I patted the seat..."

"Okay..." Alice said as she smiled and sat down. Sergeant Hurley sat across from her, next to Beautiee...

"Welcome to Longhorn Steakhouse – can I start you off with something to drink?" the waitress asked...

"Henney for me..." Bazil said...

"Long Island Ice Tea..." Beautiee said...

"Ginger ale for me..." Sergeant Hurley said...

"You're not drinking?" Darien asked...

"I'm on the clock..."

'I'll have what he's having..." Darien said...

"Okay – another henney – how about you Maam?" the waitress asked me...

"She'll have a Long Island Ice Tea..." Beautiee answered...

"Beautiee – I'm still hung over from last night..." I laughed...

"She'll have a Long Island Ice Tea..." Beautiee repeated...

"I'll have a ginger ale..." Alice said...

"You're not drinking?" I asked...

"I'm on the clock too..." she laughed...

"You are?"

"Sho am – I don't git off work until those chi'ren go home to they Momma!" she laughed...

"Here's your drinks..." the waitress said as she started putting the drinks on the table...

"Are you ready to order?"

"Not yet..." I answered...

"You may not be ready to order – but I am!" Alice laughed...

"Alice – wait..."

"Okay..."

"I'll come back..." the waitress said as she went to another table...

"I want to make a toast to Alice – Captain of the Neighborhood Watch..." I said as I raised my glass..."

"To Alice – Captain of the Neighborhood Watch..." they all repeated as they raised their glasses and then we all took a sip...

"Thank God you were there Alice – if it weren't for you – I might've lost Lacey for good..." Darien said...

"Aww damn – y'all got me cryin' – I don't have any tissue..." Alice sniffed...

"I'll take care of that..." Sergeant Hurley said as he touched Alice on her face and wiped her tears with his thumb..."

"Thank you..." Alice said as she blushed...

"Okay – I'm hungry – let's look at this menu..." Beautiee said...

"We'll get two orders of the Wild West Shrimp and the Seasoned Steakhouse Wings..." Bazil said as the waitress came back to the table...

"Okay – I'll go place that order and then I'll be back..." she said as she walked away..."

"I'm having the Renegade Sirloin..." Darien said...

"I'm having the Outlaw Ribeye..." Sergeant
Hurley said...

"Ribeye for me..." Bazil said...

"I'ma have the buttermilk Fried Shrimp..."
Alice said...

"I'm having the Lorghorn Salmon..." I
said...

"I'm having the Longhorn Steak Tips..."
Beautiee said...

"Okay – the sides are Loaded Baked
Potato, Mac & Cheese, Mashed Potato, Sweet
Potato, Fries, Rice, & Broccoli..." Sergeant Hurley
read off the menu...

"I'm having the Loaded Baked Potato..."
Darien said...

"Loaded Baked Potato..." Bazil said...

"Mac & Cheese..." Alice said...

"Rice..." I said...

"Mac & Cheese..." Beautiee said...

"I guess nobody wants any vegetables..."
Darien laughed...

"We're having salad – that's our
vegetable!" I laughed as the waitress came back
to the table...

"Here are your appetizers..." she said as
she put them on the table...

"Ooohhh... that looks good!" Alice
exclaimed...

"Is everybody ready to order?"

"Yes Maam!" Alice exclaimed as we all
laughed...

"Okay – caesar salad – or house salad?"

"Caesar!" we all said in unison..."

"That was easy – okay – I'll get your salads..." she said and then she went to get our salads...

"I'm so happy..." Beautiee said...

"Me too..." I said...

"Me too!" Alice said...

"Okay – I'm back – and I'm ready to take your orders – go!"

"One Renegade Sirloin, Two Ribeye – with Loaded Baked Potatoes – Buttermilk Shrimp, Longhorn Steak Tips – with Mac & Cheese – and one Salmon with Rice..." Bazil said...

"Okay! I got it – I'll be back!" the waitress said as she went to place our orders...

"Thank you Bazil – you made that easy..." Darien said...

"You're welcome..."

"Beautiee – you wrote that gangster book – right?" Alice asked...

"Yes..."

"I have both of 'em..."

"Thank you – I hope you're enjoyed them..."

"Sho did – you got any more?"

"I do – Lacey – give my information to Alice..."

"Okay – I will..." I said ad the waitress came back with the food...

"Okay – hope you're hungry!" the waitress said as she started putting the food on the table...

"Oh my goodness – look at this!" Alice exclaimed...

"Will there be anything else?"

"Yes – can you get a picture?" Beautiee asked as she took her phone out...

"Sure..." the waitress said as Beautiee passed her phone down and then the waitress took a few pictures...

"I want one!" I said...

"Me too!" Alice said...

"I'll send it to Lacey..." Beautiee said...

"Can you send it to me?" Sergeant Hurley asked...

"I sure can..." Beautiee answered as she sent it to him...

"Here Alice – look..."

"Oh that's nice!"

"It sure is..."

"Can everybody hold hands?" Beautiee asked. We all held hands... "Lord – we thank you – amen!"

"Amen!" we all said in unison and then we ate, drank, laughed, and talked.

Chapter 18

"Bye!"

"See you later!"

"I had fun!"

"We gotta do this again!" we all said to each other followed by hugs and then we all went to our cars...

"Alice?"

"Yes Jeremy?"

"I have a really nice time with you..."

"I had a nice time too..."

"Next time it'll be dinner – and I'll make sure it's just the two of us..."

"Next time?"

'I'd like to see you again – if that's alright..." Sergeant Hurley said as he leaned in to kiss Alice...

"Oh that's fine..." Alice breathed...

"The kiss? Dinner? Or me?"

"All that!" she laughed. Sergeant Hurley leaned in to kiss Alice again and this time, he pulled her close, wrapped his arms around her, and held her...

"Oh Jeremy... it's been so long..." she breathed...

"It's been a long time for me too..."

"Really?"

"I haven't been with a woman in about two years..."

"Why?"

"I haven't wanted anyone since my wife died... but then I saw you..."

"I was cussing that man out something terrible..."

"I don't care about that..."

"You don't?"

"I like your fire..." Sergeant Hurley said as he kissed her again...

"My husband used to tell me that..." she sighed...

"I'm sorry..."

"No... it's okay – I'm glad you like my fire – most men don't..."

"I'm not most men..." Sergeant Hurley said as he kissed her again...

"Jeremy... I need to get back home..."

"I'll get you back home..." Sergeant Hurley said as he started the car...

"I love you..." I said as I turned to Darien...

"I love you too..."

"I can't wait to get home..."

"You're ready to try out the camera – aren't you?"

"Yea..."

"About that..."

"Yes Darien?"

"I was thinking maybe we could go to Grand Pequot Tower at Foxwoods..."

"Oh Darien!" I exclaimed...

"I'll get a room..." Darien said as he smiled at me mischievously. I watched Darien get the reservation and then he started the car... "We're all set..."

"I can't wait..." I sighed...

"You haven't been punished in a while..." Bazil said as they got in the car...

"I've been too busy to be naughty..." Beautlee laughed...

"Don't you miss your Thirst Quencher?"

"Hmmm... you know... now that you mention it... I do miss him..."

"Would you like to see him when you get home?" Bazil asked as he smiled at her mischievously...

"Yes – I'd like him to come visit me..." she answered as she smiled back at him mischievously...

"I need to tell you something..."

"Okay..."

"Before I met you – I worked as an escort..."

"Oh my God!" Beautiee exclaimed...

"This was before I thought about starting my publishing company..."

"Oh so you were in your 20's..."

"Yea..."

"Why didn't you tell me this before?"

"I don't know – but I'm telling you now – because..."

"Tell me..."

"When I serviced women..."

"You were their Thirst Quencher..." Beautiee sighed...

"Are you upset?"

"No..." she answered as she smiled...

"When I saw you at the hotel... and I told you I was your Thirst Quencher..."

"Bazil?"

"Yes Beautiee?"

"You gave me my life back that night..."

"You gave me my life back too..."

"You are my Thirst Quencher..." she sighed as she took his hand...

"I love you so much..." Bazil said as he teared up...

"Bazil... don't cry..." she said as she pulled Bazil into a kiss and kissed him hard...

"You're home..." Sergeant Hurley said as they pulled up...

"I know..." Alice sighed...

"What's wrong?"

"I wanna stay with you..."

"Awww... Alice... that's so sweet... thank you..."

"You're welcome..."

"Can I kiss you?" he asked...

"I want you to... but I don't want them all in my business..."

"I don't care if you don't..." Sergeant Hurley said as he leaned in and kissed her before she could object...

"Ummm... I guess they know now..." Alice sighed...

"What time do you get off work?"

"I get off at 5..."

"I'll pick you up at 6..." he said as she got out the car...

"I'll see you at 6!" she said as Sergeant Hurley drove off...

"Uh uh – where you goin'?" Shirley asked...

"I'm goin' upstairs..."

"You got to give me details!" she exclaimed as she snatched Alice by the arm...

"You want details?"

"You know I do!"

"He kiss better than Darien..." she said and then she went upstairs...

"Are you here to check in?" the concierge clerk asked...

"Yes we are..." Darien answered...

"Name please..."

"Mr. & Mrs. Beaufort..."

"Mr. Beaufort – okay – I just need a card for incidentals..."

"Here you go..." Darien said as he handed her the card...

"Thank you – here's your room key – go down the hall, make a left, and when you get off the elevator – make a right..."

"What time is check-out?" I asked...

"Check-out is 12 p.m. – late check-out is 1 p.m...."

"Thank you..." I said as Darien took my hand and led me down the hall to the elevator...

"What room are we in?"

"732..."

"We'll have a nice view off the deck..."

"Yes we will..." Darien said as the door opened and we got off the elevator... "Come with me..." Darien said as he took my hand and led me down the hall to our room...

"Daddy! Mommy!" the kids squealed when they saw us...

"You're home? Already?" Beautiee asked...

"Yes Mommy!"

"You forgot they had a half-day today huh?" Keisha asked...

"Oh shoot – that's right!"

"Mommy – can I stay here and play?" Amina asked...

"Y'all feel like being bothered?" Keisha asked...

"She's no bother..." Bazil answered...

"Okay – bye!" Keisha laughed as she got up and left. Bazil pulled Beautiee into a kiss and whispered... "Tonight..." in her ear...

"Hey" Alice said as she got in the car..."

"Hey..." Sergeant Hurley said as he started the car and drove. Alice didn't say anything as they rode – she just looked out the window. Sergeant Hurley looked over at her and smiled. When they got to his house, she was in shock...

"Oh my God! This nice!"

"Thank you..." Sergeant Hurley got out the car, opened the door for her, and helped her out...

"Thank you..."

"Come with me..." he said as he took her by the hand and led her into the backyard...

"This is huge! I could have a nice barbeque back here!"

"You could..."

"You take care of this by yourself?"

"I do..."

"Oh wow – you have a nice deck!"

"Thank you..."

"You ever sit on the deck at night?"

"Not since my wife died..." he sighed...

"I'm sorry..."

"That's okay – c'mon – I'll take you inside..." he said as he took her by the hand and they walked around to the front door. Sergeant Hurley let Alice in and she was in shock again...

"Oh my God! This nice!"

"Thank you – let me take your coat – make yourself comfortable..." he said as he helped Alice out of her coat...

"Can I look around?"

"Of course..." Alice walked from the living room, to the family room, to the kitchen, and then she walked into the bedroom. Sergeant Hurley was right behind her... "I can't wait to make love to you..." he breathed as he began kissing her on her neck...

"Jeremy... wait..."

"Don't you want me?" he asked as he continued kissing her on her neck...

"I want you... but..." Jeremy turned her around and kissed her...

"You're not ready..."

"You mad?"

"No Alice – I'm not mad..."

"It's been a long time..."

"C'mon – come keep me company while I make you dinner..." he said as he took her hand and they went into the kitchen.

Chapter 19

"My Thirst Quencher," Beautiee breathed as Bazil pulled her into a deep, passionate kiss... "I missed you so much..."

"Come with me," Bazil commanded as he took her by the hand and led her to the bed... "Take off your clothes..." Bazil commanded. Beautiee did as she was told... "Come here to me..." he commanded as he watched her walk towards him... "Undress me... slowly..."

"Yes my Thirst Quencher," she said as she began undressing him. Beautiee took her time sliding his shirt off his shoulders and down his arms... "Damn you smell good," she moaned as she began kissing him down his chest...

"Stop..." Bazil commanded... "Go sit on the edge of the bed..."

"Okay!" she squealed. Beautiee did as she was told, sat on the bed, and watched Bazil come towards her. Once he was standing in front of her he picked her head up by her chin...

"Who am I?"

"My Thirst Quencher..." she breathed. Bazil unbuckled his belt, dropped his pants, and stood before her with his dick directly in front of her...

"Open your mouth..." he commanded. Beautiee did as she was told..."Quench your Thirst..." he commanded as he slowly placed his dick in her mouth... "Yeeesss.... Beautiee..." Bazil moaned as she quenched her thirst... "Mmmm... Mmmmmm..... That's it... suck it..." he moaned as he grabbed her by the head and pushed his dick in deeper... "I'm about to cumm.... Beautiee.... Beautiee..." he moaned as she swallowed him... "Shhiittt.... Fuck.... Fuck... Fuck.... Aaaaaaggghhhh!" He continued to stand there and let her suck his dick for a few moments until he spoke... "I'm not done with you..."

"I know..."

"Lay back... and spread your legs..."

"Yes my Thirst Quencher..." she breathed as she did as she was told...

"Mmmmmm..." he moaned... "Look at my pretty pussy..." he breathed as he slid two fingers inside her, pulled them out, and licked them... "Damn you're so wet..." he breathed as he got on his knees, slid his hands under her ass, pulled her to the edge, spread her legs... and dove in...

"Oh Bazil..." she moaned as he swirled his tongue inside, then spread her lips and began sucking... "Bazziiiilll!" she screamed as she arched her back and came in his mouth... "Mmmmmm... you taste so good..." he breathed as he continued licking and sucking...

"Bazil... Bazil... Bazil..." she moaned as he slid his hands under her ass and buried his head further and his tongue deeper... "Aaaagggghhhh.... Aaaagggghhhh.... Aaaagggghhhh!" she screamed before collapsing on the bed. Beautiee watched as Bazil stood up, climbed up on the bed, and lay on top of her...

"Taste yourself..." he commanded as he pulled her into a deep kiss, slipping his tongue inside as he covered her mouth completely...

"Mmmmmm......" she moaned as she enjoyed the taste and he began pounding her pussy...

"Bazil... Bazil... Bazzziiilll!" she screamed...

"Yessss Beautiee... who's... pussy... is... this..."

"Yooouuurrrsss!" she screamed as she came again. Bazil continued thrusting until her orgasm subsided and then got up off of her...

"Get up and turn your ass towards me..." he commanded. Beautiee did as she was told and as she did, she could feel the tip of Bazil's dick on her ass... "Grab the headboard and hold on..." Bazil commanded... "Spread your legs..." Bazil commanded... "May I?" Bazil whispered in her ear as he slipped on a condom and lotioned it with Vaseline....

"Yeeesss..." she breathed as he began playing with her pussy...

"Ooohhh... that feels good..." she moaned as he slowly began inserting himself in her ass...

"Mmmm Mmmm..." she moaned as he continued playing with her pussy while going in further...

"Are you okay?" he asked as he began thrusting...

"Oh Bazil..." she moaned as she began to enjoy sensations from Bazil indirectly hitting her G spot. Bazil stopped playing with her pussy and pulled her close to him, breathing heavy in her ear, still thrusting... "Bazil... I'm gonna cummmm..." she moaned...

"I'm cumming with you Beautiee..." he growled in her ear as he began thrusting deeper...

"Bazil... Bazil... Bazil..."

"Beautiee... Beautiee.... Beautiee...."

"Aaaagggghhhh!"

"Uuuugggghhhhh!" They both collapsed on the bed while Bazil was still inside her... "Beautiee..." he whispered in her ear while kissing her neck...

"Bazil..." she moaned...

"Did you enjoy your Thirst Quencher?"

"Yeeesss..."

"Would you like to see him again?"

"Yeesss..." she moaned as he slid out her ass, took off the condom, dropped it on the floor, and spooned her until they both fell asleep...

"Are you ready?" Darien asked...

"I guess..."

"Lacey – what's wrong?"

"I... I don't know..."

"You're freaked out by the camera?"

"Yea... I'm sorry..."

"Lacey... come here..." Darien said as he pulled me into a hug...

"Please don't be mad at me..."

"I'm not mad at you Lacey..."

"I really want to..."

"Lacey – it's okay..."

"You promise?"

"Come here..." he breathed as he pulled me into a kiss...

"Mmmm..." I moaned. Darien led me backwards towards the bed as he continued kissing me and then he pushed me back onto the bed...

"Take off your clothes..." he commanded. I unbuttoned my blouse, took it off, and then removed my bra as Darien came over to me... "Stand up..." he commanded. I did as I was told. "Unbutton my shirt and take it off..." I unbuttoned Darien's shirt and took it off his shoulders. Darien pulled his t-shirt over his head, pulled me to him, and kissed me... "Take my pants off..." I unbuckled his belt, unclasped his pants, and pushed them down over his ass, taking my time as I did so. Darien kicked his pants off his feet and stood in front of me... "Sit down..." I did as I was told... "Suck my dick..."

'Yes Daddy..." I said as I took his dick in my mouth...

"Lacey..." he whispered as he began playing in my hair. I reached up, grabbed his ass, and pushed his dick in further... "Lacey... Fuck... Suck it..." he moaned as he grabbed my head and began fucking my mouth... "Lacey... Lacey... Lacey..." I relaxed my jaws and he continued fucking my mouth as the tip of his dick touched my tonsils... "LACEY! FUCK! I'M CUMMING! UUGGHH!" I swallowed every drop and looked up at him as I continued sucking... "Lacey... Ohhh... Lacey..." I continued sucking until Darien stopped me... "Stand up..." I did as I was told. Darien pulled me close to him, pushed my pants and my panties down off my waist and over my ass, and then he began sucking and squeezing my breasts...

"Oh Darien... that feels so good..." Darien stopped abruptly and knelt down...

"Don't move..." he breathed as he dove in...

"Darien! Haah... Haah... Haah..."

"Yes... That's it..." Darien breathed and then he went back to devouring me...

"Darien..." I moaned as I grabbed his head... "Oh God... Yes... Don't stop..." Darien continued licking and flicking his tongue up and down and I was close to cumming... and then he stopped...

"Get on your back... he commanded. I did as I was told. Darien got on his knees... spread my legs apart, and dove back in...

"DARIEN! OH GOD! I'M CUMMING!" Darien continued licking, sucking, and slurping as I enjoyed multiple orgasms until I couldn't take it anymore... "Darien... I'm... sensitive..." Darien stood up and looked down at me lovingly. I looked back at him and admired my juices all over his lips and chin...

"Get on your back..." I did as I was told. Darien spread my legs, lay on top of me, and eased himself inside me and began fucking me slowly at first...

"Darien... Fuck me..." I moaned...

"You want this dick?" he asked as he held me by my waist, pushed his dick in further, and I felt his balls smacking against my pussy as he fucked me harder...

"Yes Darien! Yes! Fuck me!"

"Whose pussy is this?" he growled as he continued pounding my pussy...

"Yours! Oh God! Yours!"

"Gimmie that pussy!" Darien growled as he continued pounding...

"DARIEN! I'M CUMMING!"

"CUM FOR ME!"

"AAGGHH! AAGGHH! AAGGHH! AAGGHH! AAGGHH!"

"UUGGHH! UUGGHH! UUGGHH! UUGGHH! UUGGHH!"

"Oh Darien..." I moaned. Darien pulled out of me and stood up...

"Smells good..." Alice said as she sat down...

"I remembered you like shrimp..." Sergeant Hurley said...

"You makin' Shrimp? What else you makin'?"

"Uh uh uh..."

"Okay... I'll wait..." Alice watched as Sergeant Hurley continued cooking. He started humming and it made her smile... "My Momma used to hum when she cooked..."

"It drives my mother crazy..." he laughed as he opened the oven and took out the shrimp..."

"Ooohhh! Is that garlic parmesan roasted shrimp?"

"Yes..."

"Oh my God – you can cook!"

"What would you like to drink?"

"I'd like one of them Long Island Ice Teas..."

"I can make that..."

"Okay..." Alice watched as Sergeant Hurley went into the cabinet, took out Triple Sec, Captain Morgan rum, Vodka, Tequila, and Gin... "You a bartender too?"

"When I need to be..." he answered as he made her the drink and handed her the glass... "Taste it..."

"Ooohhh... this real good..."

"Go sit outside – I'll bring the food..."

"Okay..." Alice said as she went outside and sat down. Sergeant Hurley made the plate inside and then he brought her plate out first... "Oh wow!"

"You're welcome..." he laughed. Alice looked at her plate of garlic parmesan roasted shrimp with baked macaroni & cheese, steak, and Caesar salad as Sergeant Hurley went inside to get his plate. When he came back out, he put his plate on the table and turned to go back inside...

"Where are you going?"

"I'm going to get my drink – I'll be right back..." Alice waited for Sergeant Hurley to come back and then he sat down to eat...

"Taste it..." he said...

"This better than Longhorn Steakhouse!" she exclaimed as they ate...

"I'm glad you're enjoying it..." They both finished their good without speaking. When they were finished, Sergeant Hurley got up, took the dishes inside, came back outside, pulled Alice close to him, and they both finished their drinks as the sun went down...

"Are you ready?" he asked...

"Yes... I'm ready..."

"Okay – I'll take you home..."

"I don't wanna go home..."

"I thought you said you were ready?"

"I'm ready..." she said as she pulled him into a kiss... "for you to make love to me..." she breathed as she kissed him again. Sergeant Hurley took Alice by the hand, opened the door, led her inside, closed the door behind them, and led her into the bedroom...

"Get on your hands and knees..."
"Yes Daddy..." I breathed as I did as I was told. Darien eased himself in my ass and I started to moan... "Oooohhh..."
"Am I hurting you?"
"Nooo..."
"Are you sure?"
"Yeesss..."
"Is it good?"
"Yeesss..."
"Tell me to fuck your ass..."
"Fuck my ass..." I moaned. Darien spread my cheeks so he could watch his dick going in and out...
"Fuck... Lacey..."
"Darien..." Darien grabbed me by my ass and began pounding my ass...
"Lacey... Lacey... Lacey... LLLAAACCCEEEYYY!!!" he yelled as he pulled out and shot his cum all over my ass. I stayed on my hands and knees as he rubbed his cum all over my ass and then he got on the bed, pulled me down beside him, and kissed me hard... "I love you so much Lacey..."

"I love you too..."

"Damn that was good..." he breathed...

"I'm sorry the camera wasn't on..." I breathed...

"The camera was on..."

"Oh my God! It was?"

"Yeesss..."

"Can we watch it?"

"Yeesss..."

"Oh Jeremy..." Alice moaned...

"Alice... Uuugh..."

"Haah... Haah... Haah... Haah..."

"Uuugh... Uuugh... Uuugh... Uuugh..."

"Jeremy... I'm 'bout to come... Haah..."

"Uuugh... Uuugh... Uuugh... Uuugh..."

"Jeremy... Jeremy... Jeremy... JJEERREEMMYY!"

"Alice... Uuugh... Alice... Uuugh... Alice... Uuugh... AALLIICCEE!!" Sergeant Hurley continued to lay there inside her and kissed her eyes and then her lips... "Stay with me..."

"I can't..." she breathed in between kisses...

"I'll... make... sure... you... get... home..."

"I... gotta... be... home... for...my..."

"What time do you start work?"

"7..."

"I start work at 8 – I can get up at 5 – we can leave by 6..."

"Where's your phone?"

"Here..." Sergeant Hurley said as he handed Alice his phone..."

"Shirley?"

"Alice – you alright?"

"Can you put the kids on the bus for me in the morning?"

"You wit' that Sergeant?"

"Shirley!"

"Okay, okay – I'll make sure I get the kids..." she laughed...

"Thanks..." Alice said as she hung up...

"Give me the phone..." Sergeant Hurley said...

"Here..."

"Nelson..."

"Hey Sarge – you good?"

"I'm taking PL..."

"Okay Sarge – I'll put you out – see you Friday..."

"Now... where were we?" Sergeant Hurley breathed as he took Alice in his arms and they went back to kissing.